The Outspoken Princess
and
The Gentle Knight

The Outspoken Princess

and

The Gentle Knight

A TREASURY OF MODERN FAIRY TALES

Edited by Jack Zipes

Illustrated by Stéphane Poulin

BANTAM BOOKS

NEW YORK   TORONTO   LONDON   SYDNEY   AUCKLAND

THE OUTSPOKEN PRINCESS AND THE GENTLE KNIGHT

A Bantam Book / December 1994

All rights reserved.

For permissions, please see page 225.

Introduction and Biographies Copyright © 1994 by Jack Zipes

Illustrations Copyright © 1994 by Stéphane Poulin

Book design by Glen M. Edelstein

Library of Congress Cataloging-in-Publication Data

The Outspoken princess and the gentle knight : a treasury of modern
fairy tales / edited by Jack Zipes ; illustrated by Stéphane Poulin.

p.   cm.

ISBN 0-553-09699-0

1. Fantastic fiction, American.   2. Fairy tales—Adaptation.

I. Zipes, Jack David.

PS648.F3098   1994

813'.0876608—dc20   94-781

CIP

Published simultaneously in the United States and Canada

Bantam Books are published by Bantam Books, a division of Bantam Doubleday Dell
Publishing Group, Inc. Its trademark, consisting of the words "Bantam Books" and the por-
trayal of a rooster, is Registered in U.S. Patent and Trademark Office and in other countries. Marca Registrada. Bantam Books, 1540 Broadway, New York, New York 10036.

PRINTED IN THE UNITED STATES OF AMERICA

FFG   0 9 8 7 6 5 4 3 2 1

To My Daughter
Hanna

CONTENTS

INTRODUCTION

IN DAYS OF OLD, FOLKLORISTS LIKE THE BROTHERS GRIMM compiled collections of fairy tales by recording the words of gifted storytellers and by discovering unusual stories in rare books and manuscripts. Thanks to the Grimms and other diligent nineteenth-century scholars, we now have a plethora of fairy tales from countries around the world. Over the course of time, these fairy tales have become the major staple in the early cultural experience of our young, both in book format and film. Indeed, children are introduced to the world of reality through the world of fantasy. It is a tradition that is kept alive by adults, for once touched by the fairy tale as children, we cannot help but return to its magic throughout our lives.

There are some problems with this magic, however. For instance, we usually recall just a small sampling of the classical tales of our childhood—mainly those by the Brothers Grimm, Hans Christian Andersen, Charles Perrault, and the cinematic or printed versions of Walt Disney. In fact, it often appears as if we do not have remarkable contemporary writers and tellers of fairy tales. Nor do we pause to think that many of the tales that have become part of the classical canon like "Snow White," "Sleeping Beauty," and "Cinderella" may have dubious messages when it comes to the depiction of gender roles, violence, and democracy. Since we tend to internalize the values we were exposed to as children without seriously questioning them, there is a danger that we may perpetuate the cultural and political messages of traditional fairy tales rather than seek out tales more appropriate to the social temper of our times.

Certainly I am not suggesting that we ban or censor the creations of Perrault, the Grimms, Andersen, or Disney. However, it is just as important to collect and preserve the best of the fairy tales written or told in the present period as it is to venerate the classics. We live in an age when nuclear catastrophes may at any time devastate huge regions of the globe, when senseless and cruel wars continue to be waged despite the end of the Cold War, and when children must be made aware practically from birth that danger and violence lurk around every corner. Fairy tales project utopian visions that provide imaginative escapes from the stress of these tumultuous conditions. Contemporary fairy tales not only are a refuge against the world's inhumanity, but indeed are born out of protest against such inhumanity.

The present anthology is based on this assumption.

Ever since World War II, technological and social changes have occurred at such a rapid pace and shaken our traditional value system to such an extent that the classical fairy tales have been surpassed. They continue to provide glimpses of happy heterosexual marriages, stable class systems, and successful heroes with wealth and power that may have been satisfactory for patriarchal world orders, but they offer very little hope for change in view of present-day conditions and upheavals. Even the inventive fairy-tale films Walt Disney created between the late 1930s and the early 1950s such as *Snow White* and *Cinderella* are already passé—mere souvenirs of nostalgia rather than utopian projections of new possibilities. To a certain degree, ever since the traumatic divide of World War II, we have sensed that Disney's classical fairy tales were already part of a never-never land of escape. The best of our postwar writers and artists, I believe, have responded to Disney and the anachronistic messages and images of the classical tales by seeking to reorient our utopian drives and perspectives through provocative and often stunning fairy tales of their own.

Utopia is generally defined as no place that we have ever truly seen but a place that we envision out of our dreams, yearnings, and needs. Therefore, it constantly shifts its shape and meaning depending on the real conditions of our society. Until 1945 visions of this ideal "no place" fueled an optimistic belief in nationalism and technological progress. But the Holocaust and the atomic bomb made us see that utopian desires and drives could actually be perverted by Fascists and Communists for totalitarian purposes. Soon thereafter, the Cold War, the Korean War, the civil rights movement, and the Vietnam War also compelled us to realize that what we had envisioned as a type of "manifest destiny" of American and British democracy was riddled by hypocrisy, deceit, injustice, and inequality. In the process of these sobering if not shocking experiences, writers began searching for new means to redefine utopia through the fairy tale.

Many readers have not been aware of how rich the contemporary fairy-tale tradition in America and Great Britain has been since 1945 because there have been very few collections that demonstrate how significant the different experimentations with the classical models have been. The present volume is a modest step in this direction, containing a representative selection of what I call "crossover" fairy tales written by American and British authors between 1950 and today for both young and adult readers. These unique tales crisscross age lines and historical lines leading us from the turbulent times that have followed World War II into imaginative realms where we can conceive of possibilities for humanitarian change in the twenty-first century.

Catherine Storr seeks to revise our notions of traditional fairy tales. In "Little Polly Riding Hood" (1955), part of a splendid series of tales about an ingenious young girl, she not only reverses gender roles but also comments on the danger of taking the old tales like "Little Red Riding Hood" too literally.

If Storr, who has written a number of remarkable books

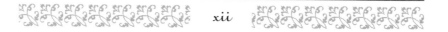

for young readers, began taking the Grimms' name in vain during the 1950s, Richard Schickel, who published an important critical study of Disney's films entitled *The Disney Version* (1968), showed equal disdain of the typically charming Disney protagonists in the 1960s. Schickel's "The Gentle Knight" (1964) mocks our ingrained expectations of a dashing hero and passive heroine with delightful wit that recalls Kenneth Grahame's droll style in "The Reluctant Dragon."

It might surprise many readers to discover that Ernest Hemingway actually wrote a fairy tale. In keeping with the themes of his longer works, "The Faithful Bull" (1951) is an existentialist story that features an unusual bull, it honors courage and integrity, and carries an implicit critique of its classical precursor, "Ferdinand the Bull." Moreover, it is a tale that provokes readers to rethink conventional virtues and storytelling itself.

Pacifism and feminism, the two major themes introduced by fairy-tale writers of the 1950s and early 1960s, became the touchstones for the major innovative tales that were to appear in the following years. For instance, Jack Sendak's wonderfully eccentric tale "The Signal" (1966) celebrates an intrepid young heroine who displays an uncanny knack for undermining a senseless war and restoring her brother's genius. This story was only the beginning of a wave of unusual tales with a feminist touch that dealt with serious issues of sexual oppression, child abuse, social injustice, and the Vietnam War.

Tanith Lee, the gifted British writer of science fiction

and fantasy, used the Cinderella plot as the basis for "Princess Dahli" (1972), which shows how a poor princess and prince expose the meanness and greed of the upper classes. Patricia Coombs invented a spunky girl in "Molly Mullett" (1975), who surprises her parents and gains the admiration of the king himself by ridding the royal realm of a ruthless ogre. John Gardner's "Gudgekin the Thistle Girl" (1976) is another hilarious parody of the Cinderella story, with the focus here on the cruel, overbearing stepmother, who defeats herself with her ridiculous schemes. Like many writers of the 1970s, Gardner questioned the abuse of power by the older generation of women, who could not understand the rise of the new feminist movement in America. Similarly, Lloyd Alexander wrote his famous fairy-tale novels of the 1960s, known as the Prydain Chronicles, to show how tyranny can be overthrown, and in 1977 he published "The Cat-King's Daughter" about the ridiculous nature of male authoritarian rulers. This elegant story features a king who hates cats but is compelled by his clever daughter to realize the preposterous nature of his arbitrary rule.

All the major protagonists of the most exciting fairy tales of the 1970s were female. Whether the tale was written by a man or woman, it is clear that the feminist movement in the United States and Great Britain played a great role in changing attitudes toward sex roles. For instance, Jay Williams, who included "Petronella" (1978) in a volume entitled *The Practical Princess and Other Liberating Fairy Tales*, consciously reverses roles in this comical narrative that portrays a

young girl who sets out to rescue a prince only to marry his more interesting captor. As in most of the other stories of the 1970s by Lee, Coombs, Gardner, and Alexander, the mood of Williams's tale is optimistic and the style humorous.

However, there were also writers who introduced tragic tones into their tales. For instance, Jane Yolen, whose work includes numerous mysterious fairy tales with shocking conclusions, wrote "The White Seal Maid" (1977) as a dramatic tale of emancipation in which a captured selchie eventually flees her husband. Richard Kennedy's "The Dark Princess" (1978) is a beautifully tender but sad story about the love between a blind princess and the Court Fool. While Yolen and Kennedy question many of the traditional assumptions of conventional fairy tales and reveal the dark side of life, they do not reject the basic utopian nature of the genre: Even though these tales induce a melancholy mood, there is still a sense that the characters retain their integrity and triumph in the end. Moreover, they depict how difficult it is to realize what utopia may be, therefore endowing their fairy tales with a vital moral force that compels readers to face the grave problems at the root of the cruelty and injustice in the modern world.

In recent years the struggle against the oppression of women and the struggle for self-esteem on the part of young protagonists have become the key issues in contemporary fairy tales. Yolen and Kennedy have been joined by other writers who have explored fascinating ways to incorporate commentaries about social conflicts into their tales. For example, Judy Corbalis introduces a strong, spirited young woman who loves to wrestle and drive forklifts in "The Wrestling Princess" (1986). Because of her exceptional self-confidence, an unusual prince seeks to marry her, defying the tradition of passive princesses and charming princes. In Antonia Barber's "The Enchanter's Daughter" (1987), a young woman realizes that as a child she was kidnapped and abused by an enchanter and risks her life breaking away from him to seek her true identity. On a more philosophical level, A. S. Byatt's "The Story of the Eldest Princess" (1991) is a subtle tale that explores narration as self-definition. Byatt focuses *not* on the youngest daughter, as is normally the case in traditional fairy tales, but the eldest, who learns to take her destiny into her own hands. The volume concludes with Dov Mir's emancipatory tale "The Outspoken Princess" (1992), in which another courageous princess defies her tyrannical parents and learns to speak out not only for herself but for others in a kingdom built on greed and exploitation.

The stories in this volume are only the tip of the iceberg in the realm of contemporary fairy tales. There are numerous other significant crossover tales that merit our attention such as Salman Rushdie's *Haroun and the Sea of Stories* (1990), Robin Morgan's *The Mer-Child* (1991), and Katherine Paterson's *The King's Equal* (1992), all of which address issues of sexism, tyranny, violence, and exploitation in highly imaginative and symbolical ways. No matter what their style or perspective, the authors of these innovative fairy tales share a common utopian urge that remains at the heart of the fairy-tale genre. Long before they were written down, oral fairy tales were used to provide a sense of community and endow listeners with hope that their world could be made a better place in which to live. This is still the major purpose of literary fairy tales. There is, however, a significant difference between the modern perception of childhood and the role parents play in the lives of their children today and the attitudes of previous generations.

In days of old, the Grimms believed that children were to be seen and not heard and that if you spared the rod, you would spoil the child. But it was not only the Grimms who believed that parents always knew what was best and should have unquestionable authority over their children. It was standard practice in the nineteenth and first half of the twentieth centuries to "care" for children by making certain they were sharply disciplined and trained according to rigid social and religious precepts that favored male privilege. Therefore, it is not by chance that most classical fairy tales up to World War II, including the Disney versions, conveyed moral lessons that reinforced patriarchal rule.

Since 1945 many fairy-tale writers have subverted the authoritarianism of these conservative tales by speaking out in the name of children, encouraging them to question the established order and even to defend themselves against the evils of the adult world. A half century ago who would have thought that children would need to hire lawyers and go to courts to defend their rights? Who would have thought that battered children would resort to intervention from the outside world so that they could gain some inner peace? Who would have thought that the pauperization of women and children in America and Great Britain would continue, and even worsen, throughout the 1980s and 1990s?

The outspoken fairy tales included here raise these questions and seek to resolve them in ways that may help us grasp imaginative and humane alternatives to the growing alienation and distrust between older and younger generations. Revising the classical fairy tales means revising our vision of how to create societies without abuse and exploitation. In the hope that they can keep the utopian spirit alive into the twenty-first century, these fairy tales have been collected and preserved for generations to come.

Jack Zipes
MINNEAPOLIS, 1994

Little Polly Riding Hood

CATHERINE STORR

nce every two weeks Polly went over to the other side of the town to see her grandmother. Sometimes she took a small present, and sometimes she came back with a small present for herself. Sometimes all the rest of the family went too, and sometimes Polly went alone.

One day, when she was going by herself, she had hardly got down the front door steps when she saw the wolf.

"Good afternoon, Polly," said the wolf. "Where are you going to, may I ask?"

"Certainly," said Polly. "I'm going to see my grandma."

"I thought so!" said the wolf, looking very much pleased. "I've been reading about a little girl who went to visit her grandmother and it's a very good story."

"Little Red Riding Hood?" suggested Polly.

"That's it!" cried the wolf. "I read it out loud to myself as a bed-time story. I did enjoy it. The wolf eats up the grandmother, *and* Little Red Riding Hood. It's almost the only story where a wolf really gets anything to eat," he added sadly.

"But in my book he doesn't get Red Riding Hood," said Polly. "Her father comes in just in time to save her."

"Oh, he doesn't in *my* book!" said the wolf. "I expect mine is the true story, and yours is just invented. Anyway, it seems a good idea."

"What is a good idea?" asked Polly.

"To catch little girls on their way to their grandmothers' cottages," said the wolf. "Now where had I got to?"

"I don't know what you mean," said Polly.

"Well, I'd said, 'Where are you going to?' " said the wolf. "Oh, yes. Now I must say 'Where does she live?' Where does your grandmother live, Polly Riding Hood?"

"Over the other side of the town," answered Polly.

The wolf frowned.

"It ought to be 'Through the Wood'," he said. "But perhaps town will do. How do you get there, Polly Riding Hood?"

"First I take a train and then I take a bus," said Polly.

The wolf stamped his foot.

"No, no, no, no!" he shouted. "That's all wrong. You can't say that. You've got to say, 'By that path winding

through the trees', or something like that. You can't go by trains and buses and things. It isn't fair."

"Well, I could say that," said Polly, "but it wouldn't be true. I do have to go by bus and train to see my grandma, so what's the good of saying I don't?"

"But then it won't work," said the wolf impatiently. "How can I get there first and gobble her up and get all dressed up to trick you into believing I am her, if we've got a great train journey to do? And anyhow I haven't any money on me, so I can't even take a ticket. You just can't say that."

"All right, I won't say it," said Polly agreeably. "But it's true all the same. Now just excuse me, Wolf, I've got to get down to the station because I am going to visit my grandma even if you aren't."

The wolf slunk along behind Polly, growling to himself. He stood just behind her at the booking-office and heard her ask for her ticket, but he could not go any further. Polly got into a train and was carried away, and the wolf went sadly home.

But just two weeks later the wolf was waiting outside Polly's house again. This time he had plenty of change in his pocket. He even had a book tucked under his front leg to read in the train.

He partly hid himself behind a corner of brick wall and watched to see Polly come out on her way to her grandmother's house.

But Polly did not come out alone, as she had before. This time the whole family appeared, Polly's father and mother too. They got into the car which was waiting in the road, and Polly's father started the engine.

The wolf ran along behind his brick wall as fast as he could, and was just in time to get out into the road ahead of the car, and to stand waving his paws as if he wanted a lift as the car came up.

Polly's father slowed down, and Polly's mother put her head out of the window.

"Where do you want to go?" she asked.

"I want to go to Polly's grandmother's house," the wolf answered. His eyes glistened as he looked at the family of plump little girls in the back of the car.

"That's where we are going," said her mother, surprised. "Do you know her then?"

"Oh no," said the wolf. "But you see, I want to get there very quickly and eat her up and then I can put on her clothes and wait for Polly, and eat her up too."

"Good heavens!" said Polly's father. "What a horrible idea! We certainly shan't give you a lift if that is what you are planning to do."

Polly's mother screwed up the window again and Polly's father drove quickly on. The wolf was left standing miserably in the road.

"Bother!" he said to himself angrily. "It's gone wrong again. I can't think why it can't be the same as the Little Red Riding Hood story. It's all these buses and cars and trains that make it go wrong."

But the wolf was determined to get Polly, and when she

was due to visit her grandmother again, a fortnight later, he went down and took a ticket for the station he had heard Polly ask for. When he got out of the train, he climbed on a bus, and soon he was walking down the road where Polly's grandmother lived.

"Aha!" he said to himself, "this time I shall get them both. First the grandma, then Polly."

He unlatched the gate into the garden, and strolled up the path to Polly's grandmother's front door. He rapped sharply with the knocker.

"Who's there?" called a voice from inside the house.

The wolf was very much pleased. This was going just as it had in the story. This time there would be no mistakes.

"Little Polly Riding Hood," he said in a squeaky voice. "Come to see her dear grandmother, with a little present of butter and eggs and—er—cake!"

There was a long pause. Then the voice said doubtfully, "*Who* did you say it was?"

"Little Polly Riding Hood," said the wolf in a great hurry, quite forgetting to disguise his voice this time. "Come to eat up her dear grandmother with butter and eggs!"

There was an even longer pause. Then Polly's grandmother put her head out of a window and looked down at the wolf.

"I beg your pardon?" she said.

"I am Polly," said the wolf firmly.

"Oh," said Polly's grandma. She appeared to be thinking hard. "Good afternoon, Polly. Do you know if anyone

else happens to be coming to see me to-day? A wolf, for instance?"

"No. Yes," said the wolf in great confusion. "I met a Polly as I was coming here—I mean, I, Polly, met a wolf on my way here, but she can't have got here yet because I started specially early."

"That's very queer," said the grandma. "Are you quite sure you are Polly?"

"Quite sure," said the wolf.

"Well, then, I don't know who it is who is here already," said Polly's grandma. "She said she was Polly. But if you are Polly then I think this other person must be a wolf."

"No, no, I am Polly," said the wolf. "And, anyhow, you ought not to say all that. You ought to say 'Lift the latch and come in'."

"I don't think I'll do that," said Polly's grandma. "Because I don't want my nice little Polly eaten up by a wolf, and if you come in now the wolf who is here already might eat you up."

Another head looked out of another window. It was Polly's.

"Bad luck, Wolf," she said. "You didn't know that I was coming to lunch and tea to-day instead of just tea as I generally do—so I got here first. And as you are Polly, as you've just said, I must be the wolf, and you'd better run away quickly before I gobble you up, hadn't you?"

"Bother, bother, bother and *bother*!" said the wolf. "It hasn't worked out right this time either. And I did just what

it said in the book. Why can't I ever get you, Polly, when that other wolf managed to get his little girl?"

"Because this isn't a fairy story," said Polly, "and I'm not Little Red Riding Hood, I am Polly and I can always escape from you, Wolf, however much you try to catch me."

"Clever Polly," said Polly's grandma. And the wolf went growling away.

The Gentle Knight

RICHARD SCHICKEL

CHAPTER ONE

n the days when knighthood was flowering like a weed, a good and gentle knight lived in a cozy castle in a quiet corner of a green and pleasant land.

Knights in those days all had names like Eric the Brave and William the Bold and Harold the Strong. But this knight was just called Freddy. Sometimes cruel people called him Freddy the Frightened, but no one ever called him by his real name, which was Frederick the Fierce.

Freddy did not really mind. He was more interested in being a poet than in being a knight. People laughed at him for this. They also laughed at him when he came home from tournaments all beaten and bloody and bruised.

That was especially cruel of them, for he only entered tournaments to please *them.* He knew people liked to have a knight to cheer on to victory. The trouble was that he never won any victories.

Still, he worked on his knightly skills daily, exercising until he was exhausted, and every month he rode off to take his beating in some tournament. He hardly ever complained except when he was pulling on his chain-mail. It scratched.

As time went on, the laughter of the people grew louder, and sometimes it turned to anger, especially when Freddy was seen wandering in the fields and forests, daydreaming about his poetry, when he could have been training with his sword and lance.

Things finally got so bad that hardly anyone would speak to Freddy, which made him feel very lonely.

Then one morning a peasant named Mort came running into the little village near Freddy's castle. He had one shoe on and one shoe off, and was going as fast as a man can go with one shoe on and one shoe off.

"The Dudgeon is coming, the Dudgeon is coming," he cried.

When they heard this, some people locked their doors and hid under their beds. They were terribly frightened. They had been told for years that Dudgeons were terrible monsters, although no one had ever actually seen one.

Some of the braver people crowded around Mort, asking him questions.

"Where is it?"

"How big is it?"

"What does it look like?"

"It is sitting on a rock in my yard," Mort replied, "and it is breathing fire out of its mouth and it is twenty feet tall. In fact, it must be the highest Dudgeon in the world."

The mayor of the village arrived to see what all the commotion was about. When he heard Mort's tale, the mayor said:

"My fellow citizens, leave this to me. I will see to it that our streets are made safe for women and children."

"What will you do?" everyone asked.

"I will get Freddy to slay the Dudgeon," he replied.

"He will probably write a poem about it instead," someone growled.

"He is the local knight," the mayor said firmly, "and he must have first chance at the job." The mayor was Freddy's friend and wanted him to have this opportunity to become popular again.

So the mayor and all the town's elders went to see Freddy. He was busy writing a poem. The mayor went, "ahem, ahum," and Freddy looked up.

"You wouldn't happen to know what rhymes with artichoke, would you?" he asked.

"Nothing," said the mayor, and proceeded to explain about the Dudgeon.

"There is no such thing as a Dudgeon," Freddy said when the mayor finished. "It is a mythical beast."

"Just the same," the mayor said, "it would set all our minds at rest if you'd go out and slay him."

"I'm working on a new poem," Freddy said, "and besides I don't want to kill anything. It isn't right to kill."

"It is your patriotic duty," said one elder.

"It is your duty to your friends," said another.

"Think of our wives and children," said a third.

"Think of the glory if you succeed," said a fourth.

"Think of what people will say if you refuse to go," the mayor said.

Freddy thought for a minute. It *would* be nice to be popular again. "Oh, all right," he said at last, "I'll go, but only for a little while."

Chapter Two

Freddy took out his strongest shield. Then he packed some jelly bread and some brown sugar sandwiches, a canteen of goat's milk, and a couple of books of poetry and set off on his quest.

He searched far and wide and near and narrow. He walked in a great circle, wandering through forest and field and fen, up hill and down dale, across rivers and around lakes. It was a nice walk, for Freddy loved the sound of the breeze in the trees, and the fresh smell of fields and wood-lands, and the sight of water rushing—white and foamy—over the rocks of the streams.

But after a week, he began to feel tired and discouraged. He was almost back to where he had started, and he had found no sign of the Dudgeon. Then, as he was walking up what he vowed would be his last hill, he heard a strange noise, like someone crying, but much louder than any human being ever cried.

Freddy crept through a patch of woods and came upon a clearing. Poking his head cautiously from behind a tree he saw a tall and most peculiar animal. It was sitting on the edge of a cliff, breathing fire and staring into the valley below.

"Imagine," Freddy said to himself, "Dudgeons really *do* exist."

He decided to kill the Dudgeon as quickly and as merci-fully as possible. Silently he stole up behind the strange crea-ture, raising his great sword over his head. . . .

"Go ahead. Get it over with," the beast said sadly.

Freddy was so startled at the sound of the voice that he dropped his sword.

The Dudgeon looked at Freddy out of soft, sad brown eyes. "I'm sorry I startled you," he said politely.

"Aren't you going to fight and bellow and breathe smoke and fire out of your nose?" said Freddy.

"Don't be silly," the Dudgeon said. "I am thinking of

jumping over this cliff and ending it all." He brushed away a tear with his paw. "You'd be doing me a great service if you'd make use of that sword you just dropped," he added.

Freddy was afraid the Dudgeon was up to some trick, but he seemed so miserable that Freddy thought he should find out more. He sat down next to the Dudgeon, who remained glumly silent for a long time.

Finally, Freddy said: "My name is Freddy."

"My friends call me Charley," the Dudgeon said, sticking out his paw for Freddy to shake, "except I don't have any friends."

"Is that why you were crying and thinking of jumping over the cliff?"

"Yes," Charley replied. "I'm awfully lonely."

"I'm lonely, too," said Freddy. "Why don't you tell me about it?"

Charley said that he was a special kind of Dudgeon—a High Dudgeon—and that he used to live in a land that was long ago and far away. One day some explorers discovered his group and, promising Charley untold riches and fame, persuaded him to return to civilization with them. Anxious to see more of the world, Charley agreed to go.

"That was the worst mistake I ever made," Charley sighed. "They were nice fellows, but they didn't know the first thing about sailing. The very day we set sail, they banged into some rocks and sank the boat. I was the only one to escape the wreck. I floated for days on a plank until I was washed ashore right here in your country."

"How do you like it here?" asked Freddy.

"It is a green and pleasant land, but I must say the natives aren't very friendly."

"They *are* rather reserved," Freddy agreed. "Besides, you frighten them."

"I don't see why."

"Because you go around breathing fire and smoke all the time."

Charley blushed. "I can't help it," he said.

"Why not?"

"High Dudgeons are born with an irresistible craving for hot pepper seeds. But when we eat them, we breathe fire and smoke and frighten people. We are, therefore, the loneliest creatures in the world. That is why we retired to our land which is long ago and far away."

"Have you ever tried giving them up?" Freddy asked.

"Of course! But nothing works."

Freddy tried in vain to think of some advice to give his new friend. At last he said, "Would you care for a jelly bread or a brown sugar sandwich?"

"Do you have any hot pepper seeds to sprinkle on it?" asked the Dudgeon.

"No, I'm sorry, I'm travelling light."

"Well, I'll have a sandwich anyway."

So they shared Freddy's lunch and, while eating, Freddy and the Dudgeon talked. They became so friendly that by the time lunch was over, Freddy was reciting his poems to Charley, who listened to them most politely.

CHAPTER THREE

By now Freddy had no wish to harm his new friend. But he was certain that if he let Charley go, the people of his village would never forgive him. They might even go hunting for Charley themselves and, in their fear, kill him.

"What are we going to do now?" the Dudgeon asked.

Freddy sat and thought until, suddenly, he exclaimed: "I've got it! I've got it!" He explained his plan and when he was finished, Charley clapped him on the back and cried: "You're a genius, Freddy."

They set to work immediately. Freddy took off his chain-mail and slashed it with his sword. Then he strewed it around the clearing. Charley uprooted several trees and, for good measure, scorched the ground with his breath. Then for ten minutes Charley set up a fearful howling while Freddy clanged loudly on his shield with his sword.

The plan was to make it look as if a terrible fight had taken place in the clearing, in the course of which both Freddy and Charley had fallen over the cliff and drowned in the stream below. Then Freddy and Charley planned to swim downstream and take a boat to some other green and pleasant land.

The mock battle went off splendidly. Afterwards, they walked over to the cliff and Freddy said to Charley: "You first."

Charley shook Freddy's hand, put his paw to his nose, and jumped.

As soon as Freddy saw that his friend had landed safely and was swimming strongly downstream, he, too, leaped over the cliff.

The people of the village heard the commotion Freddy and Charley made and guessed that Freddy was getting the worst of the fight. When Freddy did not return, their fears were confirmed. The mayor organized a search party and a few brave men agreed to come along and help him.

After a while they found the clearing. They looked all around for Freddy and the Dudgeon, but, of course, they were not to be found.

"They must have fallen over the cliff," one of the men said.

"Poor Freddy, he must have been braver than we thought," said another.

"Look at this mess," said a third. "It must have been a terrible fight."

"Well, time for lunch," said a fourth.

By nightfall, the men were back in the village, telling their tale. The mayor immediately organized a committee to erect a monument to Freddy. It was quickly built, because everyone felt guilty about the way he had treated Freddy.

In a little while, though, people forgot all about their hero. Only the birds paid any attention to his statue. They built nests on it, which probably would have pleased Freddy more than the monument itself.

In the meantime, Freddy's plan worked perfectly. He and Charley made their way easily to the coast, found a ship and sailed to a country they hoped would be more friendly to Dudgeons and poets.

As they sun-bathed on the deck, they thought up a plan to earn a living. As soon as they landed, they set about putting it into effect.

CHAPTER FOUR

First, they found out when and where all the country fairs were being held. Next, they bought some horses and a large wagon, in which they could both live and travel. Then they went from fair to fair, at each of them putting on an exhibition fight.

With only a little bit of make-up, Charley could make himself look just like an ordinary dragon. He would bellow, blow smoke and fire out of his nose, and generally carry on in a fierce and frightening way. Freddy would pretend to strike him with his sword (being very careful not to hurt his friend). Then Charley would pull the sword away from Freddy and they would start to wrestle about. They made an awful racket which the people thought thrilling.

Finally, Freddy would knock down Charley and the

fight would be over, and the people would applaud and throw money.

The act was most successful. Charley and Freddy loved their life, wandering the countryside, seeing new places, making new friends and, most of all, making the crowds happy.

When they saved a little money, they used it to publish a slender volume of Freddy's poetry. Then, at the end of every fight, Charley would pass through the audience selling the book as a souvenir.

Life might have gone on like this forever. But one day when Freddy was taking one of his long poetic walks in the woods, he came to a stream and on its bank he saw a lovely girl. She was reading a book and crying.

"Can I help you?" Freddy asked politely.

"Oh, there's nothing wrong," she replied. "It's just that these poems I'm reading are so beautiful that they make me cry."

"I'm interested in poetry. May I look at them?"

Freddy was amazed when he read the title of the book.

"Why—I wrote these poems," he said.

The girl, who was Princess Caroline, the daughter of a rich nobleman, was very impressed. She asked Freddy to autograph the book and then she invited Freddy and Charley to come to her father's castle for dinner.

"I get so tired of these knights who are always going around slaying dragons to impress me," she said. "Sometimes I think there aren't any really sensitive men left in the world."

She looked longingly at Freddy with her large blue eyes and he blushed and stammered most unpoetically.

Winter was coming on, and there would be no more fairs until next spring, so Freddy and Charley decided to settle down in a cottage near Caroline's castle.

Soon Freddy and Caroline were engaged to be married. They decided to spend their honeymoon touring the fairs. They even planned to include Caroline in the act. Charley could pretend to carry her off and Freddy would rescue her.

One day in March, just before the wedding, Freddy and Charley went to visit Caroline. But as they approached, they saw a great hurrying and scurrying and heard shouts of alarm.

"What's the matter?" Freddy asked her father, who was wringing his hands, pacing up and down and shouting orders at his servants.

"Caroline is gone," he said. "She has been carried off by a Great Horned Huff."

CHAPTER FIVE

Freddy knew that Great Horned Huffs were the most fearsome animals in the world. He leaped onto Charley's back and off they galloped to the mountains where the lair of the Great Horned Huff was known to be.

In time, they came to a wild and rocky pass. The wind moaned through it with a mournful sound. There they quickly found the fresh tracks of the Huff.

Freddy dismounted and, sneaking behind boulders, he and Charley went on cautiously and quietly.

Suddenly, they turned a corner and there before them stood the Great Horned Huff, slippery and slimy and smelly. Caroline lay on the ground, unconscious. The Huff was building a fire under a great iron pot. Obviously, he was preparing to gobble her up.

"Let me at him!" Charley growled.

"No. He is stronger than both of us," Freddy said. "We must be clever as well as brave."

"What will we do?" Charley groaned.

"Do you have your bag of hot pepper seeds?"

"Of course."

"Give them to me," Freddy said. "And be ready to come running if I call."

Freddy took the bag of pepper seeds, stood up, and walked casually and confidently out into the open. The Huff did not see him.

"Excuse me," Freddy said politely.

The Great Horned Huff whirled and growled.

"Excuse me," Freddy said again. "I hate to disturb you at dinner time, but have you seen a Dudgeon around here? I seem to have lost mine."

"Can't you see I'm busy?" huffed the Huff.

"Haven't seen him, eh?"

"No. Now move along, will you?"

Freddy sat down on a rock, looking very worried. "Dear me, dear me," he said. "I need him badly. You see, we have this act together and I have a booking for us. But he wandered off."

"Everybody has problems," the Huff snarled. "Now, if you'll excuse me."

"Say, I have an idea," Freddy said excitedly. Then his voice sank. "No. I suppose you couldn't do it."

"Do what? I can do anything."

"I'm sorry. I shouldn't have mentioned it. I'm sure it is quite beyond you."

The Huff was really angry now. "Tell me, tell me!" he bellowed.

"I thought maybe you would like to fill in for my Dudgeon. You look as fierce as he does. But you don't know how to blow smoke and fire out of your nose."

"I can learn. Just tell me his secret," said the Huff excitedly.

Freddy opened the bag of hot pepper seeds. "These are my Dudgeon's magic pills," he said. "You must eat the whole bag at once."

The Huff grabbed the bag, which contained at least a hundred hot pepper seeds. He gobbled them down in one mighty gulp.

His horrid face turned from green to pink to red. Then he started hopping madly about (for the hot pepper seeds burned his throat most painfully).

"Huff, huff, huff, huff, huff," cried the Huff. "Huff-puff, huff-puff, huff-puff."

Clutching his throat, he ran in a circle. Around and around he went, until he was spinning like a top.

Then the Huff gave a great leap, high into the air, shouted "Water!" and ran off to look for it, as fast as his six legs could carry him. No one ever knew if he found the water, because no one ever saw him again.

After resting a day, Caroline completely recovered from her terrible experience—and she was more in love with Freddy than ever. "You are both brave *and* clever—which is much better than just being brave," she told him. Freddy blushed.

CHAPTER SIX

Soon Freddy and Caroline were married, and, with Charley, set forth on their wanderings. In time their tours took them to Freddy's home town.

The people were surprised and delighted to see Freddy. When they heard of his great adventures, they even put fresh flowers on his statue.

Then Freddy, Caroline and Charley put on an especially good show, free, for the townspeople. When it was over, the very people who had been most critical of Freddy cheered loudest and longest, and the mayor made a speech begging all three of them to stay on. The people cheered again.

While he enjoyed show business, Freddy had to admit that travel was very tiring. Besides, his cozy old castle was right here, waiting for them.

"It's a good idea," he said, "but I have one condition."

"Yes?" said the Mayor.

"It's that you tear down that silly statue of me. It's very embarrassing."

"Done," said the Mayor.

So Freddy and Caroline and Charley settled down at last. In time, they made many friends—some of whom even came to enjoy poetry a little bit.

The Faithful Bull

ERNEST HEMINGWAY

One time there was a bull and his name was not Ferdinand and he loved to fight and he fought with all the other bulls of his own age, or any age, and he was champion.

His horns were as solid as wood and they were as sharply pointed as the quill of a porcupine. They hurt him, at the base, when he fought, and he did not care at all. His neck muscles lifted in a great lump that is called in Spanish the *morillo* and this *morillo* lifted like a hill when he was ready to fight.

He was always ready to fight and his coat was black and shining and his eyes were clear. Anything made him want to fight and he would fight with deadly seriousness exactly as some people eat or read or go to church. Each time he fought to kill and the other bulls were not afraid of him because they came of good blood and were not afraid. But they had no wish to provoke him. Nor did they wish to fight him.

He was not a bully nor was he wicked, but he liked to fight as men might like to sing or be the King or the President. He never thought at all. Fighting was his obligation and his duty and his joy. He fought on the stony high ground. He fought under the cork oak trees and he fought in the good pasture by the river. He walked fifteen miles each day from the river to the high, stony ground and he would fight any bull that looked at him. Still he was never angry.

That is not really true, for he was angry inside himself. But he did not know why, because he could not think. He was very noble and he loved to fight.

So what happened to him? The man who owned him, if anyone can own such an animal, knew what a great bull he was and still he was worried because this bull cost him so much money by fighting with other bulls. Each bull was worth over one thousand dollars and after they had fought the great bull they were worth less than two hundred dollars and sometimes less than that.

So the man, who was a good man, decided that he would keep the blood of this bull in all of his stock rather than send him to the ring to be killed. So he selected him for breeding.

But this bull was a strange bull. When they first turned him into the pasture with the breeding cows, he saw one who was young and beautiful and slimmer and better muscled and

shinier and more lovely than all the others. So, since he could not fight, he fell in love with her and he paid no attention to any of the others. He wanted only to be with her, and the others meant nothing to him at all.

The man who owned the bull ranch hoped that the bull would change, or learn or be different than he was. But the bull was the same and he loved whom he loved and no one else. So the man sent him away with five other bulls to be killed in the ring, and at least the bull could fight even though he was faithful.

He fought wonderfully and everyone admired him and the man who killed him admired him the most. But the fighting jacket of the man who killed him and who is called the matador was wet through by the end, and his mouth was very dry.

"*Que toro mas bravo,*" the matador said as he handed his sword to his sword handler. He handed it with the hilt up and the blade dripping with blood from the heart of the brave bull who no longer had any problems of any kind and was being dragged out of the ring by four horses.

"Yes, he was the one the Marqués of Villamayor had to get rid of because he was faithful," the sword handler, who knew everything, said.

"Perhaps we should all be faithful," the matador said.

The Signal

JACK SENDAK

BEHIND THE CLOSED DOOR

t will be bright and sunny again tomorrow,"
decided Gitel, looking up at the sky. She had
been walking for three days and her hair was
already down to her shoulders. She brushed it
back. The genius would know what to do. She
would be in the village very soon.

As she walked through the green valley carrying Chakino
in his cage, she came upon a fat little man leaning against a cannon. The man was yawning and trying his best to stay awake.

"What are you doing?" asked Gitel.

Yawning—"Guarding this cannon, that's what I'm doing."

"What for?"

"What for? What for? I am waiting for the signal, that's what for."

Gitel set down the cage. "What kind of signal?" she asked.

"How should I know?" replied the man, rubbing his eyes. "But I will know it when it comes."

"What happens then?"

"Why, then"—yawning—"I fire this cannon. Right at that village over there"—pointing.

"Why?"

"Why? I don't know why. My orders are to fire at that village. I am a soldier. A soldier must always follow orders."

"Where is your uniform?"

The man blushed slightly. "I forgot to take it along. It is such a pretty one too. Large brass buttons, blue jacket—"

"Are there more soldiers here?"

"Oh, yes, many. All waiting to attack. All waiting for the signal."

"Do the people in the village know about this?"

"Oh, no. It is going to be a surprise."

Gitel examined the cannon. "It seems to me," she said, "that one shot and this cannon will fall apart. It is very old."

The soldier chuckled. "What do you know about such things, you silly girl."

Gitel shrugged. She looked around her. Now she could

see the other soldiers. Hiding behind trees, under bushes, beneath camouflaged blankets. They wanted to surprise the village all right. The genius lived there and that was where she was going. She wondered if they would try to stop her.

"I must be on my way now," she said. But the fat soldier didn't hear. He was fast asleep. Gitel picked up the cage and started down the road. The other soldiers were so busy hiding that they didn't even see her.

WHEN SHE ARRIVED at the village she saw a man dangling by a rope from the top of a high steeple.

She shouted up to him, "Can you tell me where the genius lives?"

The man looked down. "What did you say?"

"I said, can you tell me where the genius lives?"

"I can't hear you. Wait. I shall come down."

The man lowered himself by the rope and soon he stood beside the girl.

"What were you doing up there?" asked Gitel.

"I was fixing that clock. It hasn't been working right lately, but I think I've got it ticking just fine now. What can I do for you?"

"I wanted you to tell me where the genius lives."

"You are trying to upset me."

"Upset you?" said Gitel. "But no. I just wanted to know where—"

"No. No. You are trying to upset me," cried the man,

tears rolling down his cheeks. "He was going to fix that clock but—but—"

"But what?" asked Gitel.

Just then the clock struck three and one of its hands fell off. It began to toll on and on and on. The man walked away weeping and the clock clanged one hundred and thirty times before the bell finally broke.

Gitel went on her way until she came to a man shoveling dirt.

"Why are you digging that hole?" she asked.

"I'm not digging a hole," said the man.

"But you are."

"No. I'm just throwing some dirt under my house."

"Why are you doing that?"

"Well, you see, there is something wrong with this house. Wasn't built right, I guess. Always keeps tipping over to one side. Figure if I throw some dirt under it, it will sort of brace it up."

"I doubt if that will do any good," said Gitel.

The man snickered. "What would you know about such things."

Gitel shrugged. "Can you tell me where the genius lives?"

The man looked at her angrily. "The genius? He was going to help me fix this house, until—"

"Until?"

The man shook his head and would not answer. Instead, he walked into his house and slammed the door behind him.

The house fell over on its side.

Gitel walked over to a bench and sat down. She looked at Chakino. Poor raven, he looked so cramped and uncomfortable in his cage. She remembered when she first found him, a tiny little thing, wretched and starving. It was only after she had put him into this cage that he began to thrive. Apparently he felt safe there—he seemed happy. Very rarely did he come out, and so he never learned to fly.

She opened the door of the cage and put her finger inside. The bird gently nipped at it. "Chakino. Chakino," said the girl, "what should I do? Shall I tell these people about the soldiers out there, ready to pounce on them? Maybe these people are bad and deserve what they are going to get, I don't know. But then, maybe it is the soldiers who are the evil ones, attacking for no good reason at all." She sat there, her chin in her hand, thinking. Chakino fluttered his wings, hopped off his perch, making quite a clatter, and began to crow. The girl smiled.

Then, looking down the street, she saw a man peering through an outrageously long metal tube. He had it pointed at the sky. Gitel picked up the cage and hurried over. "What are you doing?" she asked.

"I am the weatherman," he replied, "and I am studying the clouds to see if it will rain tomorrow."

"Will it?"

"I haven't decided as yet. After all, I've only been the weatherman for a short while. It takes me a little time to decide. The genius used to do this before—before—"

"Before?"

But the man didn't answer. He was too busy studying the clouds.

"Well, keep looking through that tube," cried Gitel angrily. "Look sharp, because you will soon see not rain, but cannonballs coming out of the sky."

The man put down his tube. "What on earth do you mean?"

Gitel pushed back her hair, which now fell below her shoulders. She said, "There is a little fat soldier in the valley who is going to shoot a cannon at this village. There are a lot of other soldiers there too."

The man hesitated a moment. "You shouldn't tell stories, little girl."

"It's the truth."

"But why?"

"How should I know."

The man thought for a while. "I wonder if I should tell the others."

"I don't know," said Gitel. "That is for you to decide now." She picked up the cage and left.

As she walked down the long street, she noticed that all the houses were drab and gray and seedy-looking. There was one, however, that was painted yellow and had black shutters. She stopped in front of it. There was the number thirteen written on the door and, for some reason or other, it seemed to beckon to her. She walked right in.

The shades were drawn. A man with a little mustache

sat before a fire, hugging his knees. He did not look up as Gitel entered. She set down the bird.

"Can you tell me where the genius lives?" she asked.

The man blinked his eyes, then opened them wide. He did not answer.

"Can you please tell me where the genius lives?" she tried again.

"I heard you. You won't be able to see him."

"But I must," shouted the girl. "I've come from so far away. See my hair?" She turned around. "See how long it is? Way past my shoulders now and I only cut it three days ago. Do you think the genius could help me?"

"I'm sure he could—have."

"Could have?"

The man sighed, stood up, and began to pace the floor. "I can see that you haven't heard," he said. "I thought every-one must have known by now. The genius can't help you. He is helpless—as a baby."

"How can that be? What has happened? I saw him just three weeks ago. He flew over my village in his chair. I thought he looked right at me, he even smiled. It was then that I got the idea to come here and ask for his help."

"Yes. I can see that you haven't heard."

"Heard what?" cried Gitel explosively. "What is it that has upset all the people in this village so?"

The man paced before the fire. He had no shoes on, just plum purple socks. "Let me start at the beginning," he said. "Many, many years ago—although when I come to think of

 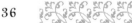

it, not so many years ago as that. The genius was not much older than you."

"Was?"

"Do you want to know where I first found him?"

"Yes, I do."

"He was an infant and I found him sitting in a tree—on top of a nest."

"What?"

"Yes. Yes. It is so. Some bird had apparently mistaken him for her chick and had placed him there. He was a tiny little thing, rather sallow, not very pretty at all, but he certainly was not a bird. It was only by sheer luck that I found him at all. I happened to be climbing trees that day."

"You were?"

"Yes. I was looking for a special tree that grows somewhere around here. A tree known to have magical properties. Oh, by the way, my name is Edvig. I am a magician."

"My name is Gitel."

"I am a magician."

"Yes, I heard you."

"I can see that you are impressed. Only, I'm not a very good one. You see, it is very difficult for me to learn new tricks or magic spells. And after I do learn them, I always manage to forget them. It is a failing of mine. But the boy I found—ah, that was a different matter entirely. He devoured my books with avidity, learning everything there was to learn. Unlike me, he would forget nothing. You see, when I brought the boy to my home I raised him as my own. I had made numerous inquiries in all of the villages as to who his parents might be, but I never did find them.

"Well, before long, after reading every book he could find in the village, the boy became expert in biology, astrology, topography, zoology, chronology, magicology, micrology, seismology, phrenology, spyology, and graphology."

"Goodness," said Gitel.

"Yes. And he concocted all sorts of things. Medicines that would cure all kinds of ills. Seeds that would grow the most fantastic flowers. Music that made everyone shiver with pleasure. And he could fix anything. And then there was his flying chair, and his magic wand, and the harp that would start to play at the snap of his finger, and—"

"His magic wand?"

"Oh, yes. You see, he found the magical tree that I was looking for. Would you believe it? It was the very same tree on which I had found him. He cut off a small branch, bathed it in a magical brew of some sort, smoked it in the flames of a magical fire—and there was his magic wand. With it he could do almost anything. Everything he wished for *himself* came true."

"I don't understand."

"Well, it would not affect others. But holding it in his hand he could become young or old, beautiful or ugly, tall or short, or even invisible."

"How wonderful!" said Gitel.

"Yes. The villagers came to love this boy genius, and he loved them in turn. Anything they asked of him, he would do. He would fly over the village in his chair, and whenever he saw anyone in trouble he would come down and help. The villagers would often come to him, seeking his advice and help, just as you did, Gitel, and he would give it freely and wisely. Sometimes he would walk through the village invisible, just to hear what the people were saying. It was in this way that he learned that they were planning to make him their king.

"He became very alarmed at this. 'I am only thirteen years old,' he said to me. 'How can I be king of all these people?' And even though I told him that he was smarter and better and more capable than anyone else in the village, that he would make a splendid king, he would not listen. He wor-

ried about it for several days. 'I am too young to be a king,' he kept insisting.

"Now, one fault the genius had was that he was always looking for signs. Whenever he wanted to do anything, he would look for some kind of an omen to prove that he was right. So one day he came to me and said that he would become king only if he got the proper sign. 'And what would that be?' I asked him. 'Oh, there are several,' he replied. If a black cat crossed in front of him on a rainy day when the sun was shining—that was one. Or if a horse happened to bark like a dog. Or if the sky turned green in the evening. Or if the leaves on the trees did not move in a windstorm. All these were important signals.

"There was another one too, but he would not tell it to me because he said it sounded so farfetched that I would not believe it anyway."

"Very, very strange," muttered Gitel. Chakino, meanwhile, was staring into a huge mirror that stood beside his cage.

"Well," continued the magician, "many, many days went by without any of the signs appearing. Each day the people would come and insist that he become king and each day the poor genius would reply that he must have a sign. At last he could stand it no longer. That night he burst into my room, his eyes red with weeping. 'My signal has not come,' he cried. 'That proves that I am not capable of being king. I would probably do more harm than good. So for the sake of the villagers I will not be a genius any longer.' And—and—right

before my very eyes, waving his magic wand, before my very eyes . . ."

The magician's voice trailed off. He stood there, staring into the fire, as though he were seeing the whole thing happening again in the flames. The raven crowed fearfully at himself in the mirror.

"What happened," whispered Gitel.

The magician turned to look at her. He said, "Before my very eyes, he was transformed into a tiny baby."

Gitel could not suppress a cry. "Oh, no. That is impossible."

"It is true," said Edvig. "It is true."

"But where is he now?"

The magician looked towards a closed door. Gitel ran to open it. Inside, in a little crib, lay a tiny baby, rather sallow and not very pretty, smiling up at the ceiling.

THE BATTLE'S TRAGIC OUTCOME

There was a great commotion outside. Edvig threw open the black shutters and he and Gitel looked out. The village was in a turmoil. People ran up and down the streets, shouting. Some gazed fearfully at the sky. Others stood in groups, wringing their hands.

A man walked by calmly, wearing a dazzling uniform.

"Who is that?" asked Gitel.

"That is General Dinklelocker," replied the magician. He called, "General, what has happened?"

The general stopped, flicked a speck of dust off his trousers, closed his eyes for several moments, put his hands behind his back, cracked his knuckles, then replied, "It appears that we are going to be attacked. We are surrounded by enemy soldiers."

"What?" cried Edvig. "How were the devils discovered?"

The general paused for a moment, then he smiled and said, "A good general is always alert to dangers. I am never caught napping."

Gitel snickered. It was she who had discovered the soldiers. But she said nothing. She noticed that there was a large rip in the back of his jacket.

"How are we to stop them?" cried Edvig.

The general took off his hat and examined it carefully. Then he put it back on and said, "We are building a wall around the village."

"That will take many days," observed Gitel.

The general did not look at her. He may not have heard her. "We have plenty of time," he said. "Our weatherman—you know what an expert he is—has predicted that there will be several days of rain. There can be no fighting until the storm is over. The wall will be finished by then."

"There will be no rain," said Gitel. "You can tell just by looking at the sky."

The general stared blankly at her. Then he turned back to Edvig and said, "Then there are the traps."

"The traps?"

"Yes," said the general, chuckling. "We are digging huge holes and covering them over with twigs and grass and such. It was my own idea. The enemy will not know they are there and they will fall into them."

"Very unlikely," said Gitel. "They couldn't be that stupid."

The general turned pale but, still speaking to the magician, he said, "It will not fail. I have had much experience in these matters, more perhaps than others who know nothing about such things."

Gitel knew that he was referring to her, but she would not be stopped. "A couple of shots from your cannons," she said, "is probably all you need to chase them off."

Edvig nodded. "That might be just the thing. Where are the cannons, General?"

The general blushed. He began to examine his shoes now. "We can't seem to find them," he said.

"What?" cried the magician.

"Well, we haven't used them for so long. No one can remember where we put them. Oh, they are quite lost." The general wiped his brow with a silk handkerchief.

"But we have our volunteers," he continued. "The bravest of our men. If all else fails, they will go forth and win the day for us." With that, General Dinklelocker walked off as grand as a peacock.

Edvig closed the blinds again and sat down before the fire. He began to tell the girl of his life as a magician and of all the wonders he had wanted to perform. But Gitel was very tired and she soon fell asleep with her arm around Chakino's cage.

THAT NIGHT GENERAL Dinklelocker received a message from the enemy. They declared that no harm would come to anyone if the genius were to be turned over to them. The general refused them coldly and the war was on.

At daybreak the sun rose shiny and warm. There was no

storm after all. The wall, which had been growing all night, was, apparently, badly constructed. It collapsed with a great roar. The cannons were never found and the brave volunteers who set out to chase the enemy away all fell into the very traps the general had ordered dug. Meanwhile, over on the other side, the sleepy soldier guarding the cannon finally did see what he believed was the signal and fired away at the village. On the first shot, though, the weapon fell apart and did damage to no one. But when the villagers heard the cannon, they became so panic-stricken that they ran to the general and demanded that he do something. He did. He sent a message to the enemy and told them that they could have what they wanted. The triumphant soldiers entered the town, smashed down the door of number thirteen, and seized the poor genius.

Gitel slept through it all.

When she finally awoke, Edvig tearfully told her what had happened.

"Look. Look," he cried, pointing out the window. "See what they are doing."

Gitel ran to look. The enemy soldiers were marching down the street, watched by the weeping villagers, dragging along behind them a huge iron cage—within which, all alone, lay the little baby.

Gitel burst into tears.

WE SHALL RESCUE HIM

"But why do they want him?" asked Gitel.

"They believe that he will grow up to be a genius again. As their prisoner, he will be forced to do their will. In this way they will grow very powerful."

"They never will—because we shall have him back."

"No, Gitel, no. It is hopeless. They are too strong for us. He is lost." The magician shook his head sadly and tapped gently on Chakino's cage.

"How could the villagers give him up?" wondered Gitel.

"We weren't prepared to fight. We did not know how to resist."

"They came in here as I slept. Why didn't you awaken me?"

"I tried to stop them. I tried magic on them. I put several spells on them, but nothing worked. The soldiers threw me to the ground. They might have hurt you had you got in their way. That is why I let you sleep."

"Well, now we must get him back," said Gitel.

"No. No. It is hopeless."

"It is not hopeless. We must think of a way. We must stop the soldiers somehow."

"How can we do that?"

"You are a magician, Edvig. Surely you must know of a powder that would, say, put them all to sleep."

Edvig wrinkled his brow. "Well, I told you that I was a

poor magician, and that was perfectly true. But I do seem to recall having once made some such powder. It worked rather well, I believe. In fact, it was one of the few things I made that worked at all."

"Could you make it now?"

"I wrote it down somewhere."

"Find it, Edvig. Oh, find it."

The magician began to thumb through his books, of which there were many. Gitel, meanwhile, sat with her chin in her hand, thinking. At last, a shout brought her to the magician's side. "Here it is," he cried. "See?"

Gitel looked at the page. It was all scratchy and scribbly and covered with many ink blots. "Oh, dear," she said, "how will you ever read it?"

"*You* will," answered the magician cheerfully. "You read the ingredients off to me and I will mix them all together."

Gitel squinted at the page and then, falteringly, began to read. It was very difficult. She read off the unfamiliar names of the various chemicals while Edvig stirred them in a huge bowl. And then, after almost giving up the whole idea, the magician finally announced that perhaps the powder was ready.

"But how can we tell for sure that it will work?" asked Gitel.

"We must try it out," answered the magician.

They both looked out the window, and there below them stood the general. He was checking his watch against the one-handed clock on the steeple.

"Shall we?" mused Edvig.

"Why not?" giggled the girl.

He took a pinch of the powder and let it drop on the general's head. The general stood stock-still for a moment and then, with a queer smile on his face, dropped to the ground and began to snore. The magician jumped for joy.

"It works," he cried. "It works. It is the first magic of mine to work in years. And I have you to thank for it, Gitel."

"Yes, but how are we to drop the powder on the soldiers? The flying chair?"

"No. No. Only the genius can make that work. I tried it once and it spun me around so that I was dizzy for days."

Gitel looked at the cage. She pursed her lips. "It will have to be Chakino then."

She opened the door of the cage and tapped on it. The raven clattered off his perch and flung himself about.

"But I thought he could not fly, since he is always in that cage," said Edvig.

"Could not? Oh, no. Would not is more like it. He is too frightened. Chakino, Chakino, will you do it for us?" She put her head close to the bird. She must have looked enormous to him.

"Are we to abandon the genius, Chakino?" she asked. "If we do, he will be lost forever."

The bird cawed.

"Does that mean yes?" cried Edvig.

Gitel laughed. "I do not know. Does that mean yes, Chakino?"

The bird cocked his head, looking at both of them. Then he retreated into the shadows of his cage.

"He is thinking it over," said Gitel. "But I know that we can depend on him."

"I hope so," said the magician doubtfully.

"Now," continued the girl, "we come to the magic wand. It made him into a baby, it will make him back into a man."

"No. No. That is impossible. I told you he constructed it so that only he could make it work. He did not want it to fall into the wrong hands."

"Yes, I know, Edvig. But the baby himself will hold it. When the soldiers are all asleep I shall put it into his hands. Then I shall make the proper wish."

"Gitel, you are mad. That will never work. It is the most unreasonable plan I have ever heard. It will not work. Besides, nothing ever works out the way it is supposed to in this village."

"Come," said Gitel, locking the door of the bird cage and picking it up. "We will have to catch up to the soldiers. We must hurry, they must have reached the valley by now."

And off they went to rescue the genius.

At Last . . . The Signal

"See? There they are, below us," said Gitel, pointing. She and Edvig were lying on their stomachs, looking down over the edge of a hill. The bird hopped onto the open door of the cage and watched.

"It will not be too difficult for Chakino," continued the girl. "He need only fly out a little way. I will tie the bag of sleeping powder to his leg and as he flies over the soldiers it will fall on them. This is the perfect spot and we've arrived just at the right time. They are directly below us now." She looked down again into the misty blueness of the valley. The soldiers were marching slowly and noisily.

"Shh, don't talk too loud," whispered the magician. "The soldiers might hear us."

"They cannot hear us all the way down there." Then, teasing, "They might see your purple socks, though." The magician dug his toes deeper into the grass.

Laughing, Gitel stood up and said, "It is time to start now. Oh, Chakino, I see you are getting ready to join us. I knew you would help." The bird looked up at her, cocking his head from side to side. He cawed loudly.

"Shh-shh," cautioned Edvig.

"Are you ready?" asked Gitel.

The bird turned to preen his tail feathers. But when Gitel attempted to tie the little bag of powder to his leg, he fled in panic to the top of Edvig's head.

"What is happening?" whispered the magician. "What is happening up there?"

Gitel laughed. "Oh, he is only picking on your hair." Then, coming near, she spoke softly to the bird. "Just let me tie this to your leg—" But the raven fled again. Fluttering his wings at great speed, he rose crazily into the air. He flew in a mad circle and then, like a stone, he fell headlong onto the grass.

"Oh, he is killed," cried the magician.

"No. No. He is all right. Try again, Chakino."

The bird looked dazedly around and then, flapping his wings at an incredible speed, rose slowly upward. But he remained in one spot as though suspended in air. Edvig waved his arms up and down in encouragement. "It looks like he is stuck," he cried. "Do you want me to throw a spell over him—to make him fly?"

"No," said the girl. "He will do it all by himself."

"It is just as well," said Edvig. "I've forgotten how to cast that particular spell anyway."

Gitel held out the palm of her hand and the bird hopped onto it. He kept his head down and nipped gently at her finger.

"It is hopeless," wailed the magician.

Gitel did not listen to him. She said, "It seems to me, my bird, that you are on the verge of success. Now, I do not know too much about flying, but I believe you are flapping your wings much too rapidly. You should do it slowly, evenly, gently—that should do it. Tie the powder to his leg, Edvig."

The magician did as he was bid and this time Chakino did not protest. Then the girl raised her arm as high as she could. The raven fluttered his wings easily and Gitel could feel his weight growing lighter and lighter. Then the bird stretched his neck and soared gracefully into the sky. Edvig clapped his hands over his mouth, stifling a cry of surprise.

Together, breathlessly, they watched the bird fly over the unheeding soldiers. Once, twice, three times he flew over them and finally the bag came loose and the powder fell on their heads. And as though they were struck by an invisible wave, the soldiers fell to the ground, fast asleep.

"Come," cried Gitel. "We must hurry."

The two dashed down the hill and past the soldiers.

The magician poked at a few of them to make certain they were asleep. They were. Then they came up to the huge cage. The baby was sleeping peacefully in it.

"Oh-oh," cried Edvig. "The powder has put him to sleep also. Oh, why didn't we think of that?"

Gitel looked at him.

"I knew your plan would not work," continued the magician. "Let us flee from here. The soldiers will soon awaken."

Chakino, sitting on top of the cage, fluttered his wings.

"I knew the powder would put the genius to sleep," said Gitel, "but that makes no difference. We can still put the wand in his hand and then make our wish."

"How are we to do that? The cage is locked. I cannot open it. How are we to put the wand in his hand if we cannot get close enough to him?"

Gitel could see that the magician was right. What could she do now?

"Some of the soldiers are stirring," whispered the magician in terror. "The powder wasn't strong enough."

Gitel looked around. The soldiers might indeed awaken at any moment.

"We are trapped," cried Edvig. "When the soldiers find us here—"

Gitel gazed up at the huge, darkening sky. Would she fail, after all? Quietly, she said, "Give me the wand, Edvig."

The magician, who had been carrying it all the while under his shirt, handed it over to her. It was just a thin little branch from the tree on which Edvig had first found the genius. It was very un-magic-looking.

The girl took it and she could feel, suddenly, the power of it coursing through her blood. Then, holding it aloft, she shouted, "Awaken, genius, and become as you were."

There was a tremendous clap of thunder and the evening sky turned green. Chakino flew away and the soldiers, waking, fled in terror. And before the startled eyes of the magician and Gitel stood—no longer a baby—the genius.

He looked around dazedly. "What is happening?"

Edvig was beside himself with joy. He cried, "What is happening? What is happening? I can't begin to tell you all of it." But he tried anyway and soon he had related the entire story.

The face of the genius lit up with happiness. Looking at Gitel, he said, "Why . . . you are my signal."

"Signal? I—a signal?"

The genius smiled. "Yes. You have given me the sign to go ahead."

"I came to you," said Gitel, "only because my hair grows so fast. Look at it. It is down to my ankles."

The genius laughed. "Is that the reason you came? No. No. You are the sign I was looking for. You are my beacon. My guiding light. My—"

"Be that as it may," Gitel broke in, "do you have some kind of ointment for my hair?"

The genius looked at her tumbling black hair. "Do you remember, Edvig, when I spoke to you of the omens I was looking for and of the one I wouldn't speak about because I felt you would not believe it?"

"I remember," said the happy magician.

The genius nodded. "Well, I will tell it to you now. It was that a princess with long, flowing hair, who could lull soldiers to sleep and who could teach birds to fly, would appear and awaken me from a deep sleep."

"But Gitel is not a princess," said Edvig.

The genius smiled. "She caused the magic wand to work and—"

"And that will only work," said the magician, "for you or for someone with the same blood as yours."

The genius nodded. "My sister."

"Sister?" whispered Gitel, with wonder in her eyes.

The genius took her hand. "And since I am to be a king, so you will be a princess."

Gitel was lost in thought for a while. Then she said, "My momma and poppa did speak of a son long lost."

A tear rolled down the genius's cheek. "I am that son. Come, let us return to the village."

The flying chair appeared out of the sky, the bars of the iron cage fell away, and the air was filled with the extraordinarily beautiful sound of a harp. Edvig sat in the chair with Gitel on one knee and the boy on the other. Chakino was nowhere in sight. They flew off into the night, leaving the two empty cages behind them.

✳   ✳   ✳

WHEN THEY ARRIVED at the village, the people went mad
with joy. "We knew the genius would outwit the soldiers,"
they cried.

"Yes," said General Dinklelocker, fully awake now.
"That was the last phase of my plan. I knew that the genius
would never let himself be taken."

But the genius stood up and told them that it had been
the girl, his glorious sister, who had saved him. This miraculous girl had thought of a bold plan, a bold plan that not only
proved successful in rescuing him but gave him the go-ahead
to become king. The general paled, looked wildly at the girl
and slunk off into the darkness. With a mighty roar the villagers proclaimed the genius their king.

When they were alone in the yellow house, the genius
gave Gitel the hair ointment she wanted. "This will be sure
to help you. Now, go back to your village and tell our parents
what has happened. Then bring them here to me so that they
may share in the happiness of their son the king. And when
you return, dear Gitel, we shall have many joyous days
together. We will fly over the village in our chair to tend to
the needs of our subjects. And we shall walk together, invisible, among the villagers to learn their wants."

Gitel kissed him and promised to return as soon as she
could. At the door Edvig said, "Your bird has learned to fly
and now he is gone. He will no longer live in his little cage.
Perhaps you will never see him again."

But Gitel said, "No. No. Chakino will never leave me. I loved him when he couldn't fly and now I love him all the more. He will be back."

Then, waving good-bye, she started down the road for home.

Princess Dahli

TANITH LEE

rincess Dahli's parents were very poor. They lived in a small castle and hardly ever had any new clothes.

One day the king said to the queen, "It's about time Dahli started to go to parties and balls and things. It's time she had some pretty dresses and found a nice young prince to marry."

"I know, dear," said the queen. "But I don't see how we can afford it all."

"I have written to my rich brother, King Archibald," said Dahli's father. "And I have had a letter from him today. He says Dahli may go and stay with him and his two daughters. She will have a splendid time there, I've no doubt."

When they told Dahli, she kissed them both and said

thank-you but really they shouldn't have bothered. She was very happy just living in the small castle and didn't care that much about balls and parties.

Nevertheless, she put on her best dress, which had only one patch on it, although it was rather a large one, and set off.

Unfortunately, she had to walk all the way, as there was no carriage. When she arrived, it was suppertime, and she was very tired and dusty, and everyone pointed at her rudely and laughed.

One of the maids ran up and pinched her, and said, "Doesn't it worry you that everybody's laughing at you?"

"It's not my fault," said Dahli, "if none of you has any manners."

WHEN KING ARCHIBALD saw her, he smiled in a pompous sort of way.

"Ah, Dahli," he said. "How tired you must be after your long walk. Here are my two daughters, Princess Carnatia and Princess Chrysanthia."

Carnatia kicked Dahli sharply on the ankle, and Chrysanthia pulled her hair.

"How do you do," said Dahli.

"I'm sure," said King Archibald, "you won't mind helping my dear daughters with their curls and their frocks." Actually, he thought that Dahli would make an ideal maid for the two princesses, both of whom were fat and not a bit pretty.

"Of course I'll help them," said Dahli. "They don't seem to manage too well on their own."

DAHLI WAS GIVEN a small, uncomfortable bed in one of the attics. To make matters worse, a family of mice lived in a large hole under the bed. While Dahli was hanging up her coat, they marched out and the oldest mouse tapped her on the foot.

"We hope," said the mouse, "that, as you are going to share our room, you will be very quiet and not disturb us. We are all light sleepers, so please be in bed before eight o'clock, and make sure you *never* snore."

"I am a light sleeper, too," said Dahli. "And I'm afraid I never go to bed before eight o'clock. I don't think I snore, but you never know, do you?"

The mice glared at her, stamped back into their hole, and slammed the door. The moment Dahli took off her shoes, they all banged on the wall.

For supper King Archibald and Carnatia and Chrysanthia had roast chicken, marmalade tart, and fresh yellow peaches. They gave Dahli a cheese sandwich and a cup of tea.

When everybody had finished, Chrysanthia pinched Dahli and said, "You must come and do up my hair for the evening. It takes at least an hour."

"Yes," added Carnatia, hitting Dahli with her fan. "I want you to sew some red ribbons on my ball dress. We are going to another ball tomorrow night."

Dahli thought all this was a bit much, but she smiled and said, "Of course," and followed them both meekly upstairs.

The princesses' bedrooms were simply enormous, and extremely comfortable, and nobody complained about how much noise they made. And the two princesses were very noisy indeed. They threw things at each other and at Dahli, and whenever they couldn't find a necklace or a handkerchief, they pulled out all the drawers and dropped them on the floor. They made Dahli clear up the mess while they made more mess somewhere else.

"Hurry up!" screeched Chrysanthia.

"How slow you are!" yelled Carnatia.

"Perhaps if you wouldn't throw so many of your hairbrushes at me, I might get on a bit quicker," said Dahli.

"Come and do my hair this minute!" shouted Chrysanthia. "Where is my comb? What have you done with it?"

"Here it is," said Dahli, getting it down from the picture rail.

Dahli did up Chrysanthia's hair with curlers and pins and ribbons, and Chrysanthia made an awful fuss, although Dahli didn't hurt her once. All the time Carnatia kept hitting her, and when she finished, Carnatia made her sew twenty-five red bows on her pink and mauve ball dress.

"Do be careful," screamed Carnatia. "Of course, I don't suppose you'd know what to do with a ball dress—you've obviously never had one."

"Well," said Dahli, "I've certainly never had one like this."

At last Chrysanthia and Carnatia got tired of poking her and throwing things at her and told her to go to bed.

"Oh, how badly you've done my hair," complained Chrysanthia.

"Oh, how badly you've sewn on these ribbons," complained Carnatia. "Still, I suppose it will have to do."

"Good night," said Dahli. "Sleep well."

"Go away, and don't be impertinent!" shouted the two princesses.

Dahli went up to her attic and got into bed. The mice were having a party behind the wall and making an awful din.

"Well," thought Dahli, "it seems to me that when I try to do things right, I can't please anyone at all. So I shall do them wrong for a change, and see what happens then." And she smiled herself to sleep.

✳   ✳   ✳

THE NEXT MORNING everybody was very busy getting ready for the ball.

"I want you to go out at once," said Chrysanthia to Dahli, "and do some shopping for me. Here is a list."

"And you can buy me some crystal slippers from the shoeshop," added Carnatia, giving her another list.

"Of course," said Dahli. "I was wondering if I could go to the ball with you."

"You!" shrieked Chrysanthia, red with rage.

"You!" shouted Carnatia, laughing like anything.

"Certainly *not!*" they both added.

"Why not?" asked Dahli.

"Because we say not," cried the sisters, and threw their fans.

Dahli took a basket and went into the town. Chrysanthia's list read like this:

> One large yellow plume to wear in my hair.
> A pair of silk stockings.
> A bunch of roses for me to carry.
> A golden comb.

Carnatia's list read like this:

> A pair of crystal slippers.
> Something pretty to wear in my hair.

Dahli shopped very carefully, put the things into the basket, and went back to the castle.

"Have you got everything?" demanded the sisters when she walked in.

"Oh, yes," said Dahli. "Here are your lists. You can check that I've bought all that you want."

Chrysanthia and Carnatia started to take things out of the basket, and pretty soon they began to scream.

"What's this?"

"Oh! Whatever's that?"

"Let me help you," said Dahli. "Here we are. One large yellow plum to wear in your hair."

"Plum!" cried Chrysanthia. "I said 'plume.'"

"Oh, dear," said Dahli, "I thought it was plum."

"And what are these?" wailed Chrysanthia, holding up a pair of woolen socks.

"Well," said Dahli, "I couldn't find any silk stockings, and I thought these would be all right. You see, I've never been to a ball, and I'm not sure what people wear."

"And what's this celery doing?" howled Chrysanthia.

"There weren't any roses, but I thought if you held a bunch of celery, it would go ever so well with your ball dress."

"And what's this?" screamed Chrysanthia, fishing out a honeycomb.

"I thought that was what you meant when you said a golden comb—"

Meanwhile, Carnatia was jumping up and down in rage, waving a pair of fluffy bedroom slippers and a cabbage.

"I'm so sorry," said Dahli. "They were the only slippers the man had in the shop."

"What about the cabbage?" screeched Carnatia.

"You said you wanted something pretty to wear in your hair."

"A *cabbage!*"

"Well," said Dahli apologetically, "I think cabbages are awfully pretty."

Carnatia and Chrysanthia were in such a state that they forgot to throw anything at Dahli, or even to pinch her.

AFTER LUNCH, THE two sisters said they would lie down in their bedrooms and have a rest before they got ready for the ball.

Dahli went quickly back to her attic and shut the door. Then she knelt down by the mouse hole and banged loudly on the wall. At last, the oldest mouse came out and glared at her. The mice took their afternoon nap at about this time, and after their party they were very tired. Dahli had wakened them all.

"Yes?" snapped the mouse.

"I simply had to ask you," said Dahli anxiously, "if I was quiet enough last night. I was so worried I might have wakened you."

"Yes," said the mouse, looking disgruntled. "You'll do." And he turned around to go in again.

"Oh, are you *really* sure I was quiet enough?" implored Dahli. "I took off my shoes as soon as I got in the door—"

"You were all right," said the mouse impatiently.

"I crept into bed," said Dahli. "And then I thought, oh, dear, perhaps I've wakened those poor mice up after all. I was so worried, you've no idea. I hardly slept a wink, and I—"

"We didn't hear you," said the mouse, and quickly shut the door.

Dahli waited until she thought he had gone back to bed, and then she knocked again, twice as loudly as the first time. There was an awful commotion on the other side of the wall, as all the mice shot out of bed with fright. She could hear the oldest mouse stamping back along the corridor. The door opened.

"What is it now?" demanded the mouse in an annoyed voice.

"Well," murmured Dahli, "I do hope you wouldn't just *say* I'd been quiet enough when I hadn't. I do hope you'd tell me if I'd disturbed you at all."

"Look here," said the mouse. "We are in the middle of our afternoon nap."

"Oh," said Dahli. "Oh, I'm so *sorry.* You should have said. I never dreamed—"

"That's all right," said the mouse ungraciously. "Good day." And he slammed the door.

Dahli sat back on her heels and waited until everything was quiet again. Then she knocked harder than ever. This time, a lot of other mice came to the door with the oldest mouse.

"What do you want?" growled the mouse.

"I was thinking," said Dahli. "As you're all having a nap, perhaps I could sing you a lullaby."

"No, thank you," said the mice hastily, and shut the door.

"It's the least I can do," shouted Dahli. And she began. She sang:

"Sleepy mousey, gently sleepy,
Though the night is dark and deepy,
O'er your cradle I will keepy
Watch, till dawn comes brightly leapy."

She sang very loudly and very badly. Soon the door opened again and all the mice began to troop out, carrying their suitcases.

"I'm sorry I only know one verse," said Dahli. "But I thought I could just sing it over and over again, until you went to sleep."

"We're moving," said the oldest mouse.

"Well," said Dahli, "I suppose it must be a bit cramped in here for you. Actually, there are two beautiful rooms downstairs. I'll show you."

The mice seemed a bit uncertain, but they followed her out of curiosity. She led them into the bedrooms of Princess Carnatia and Princess Chrysanthia.

"I shouldn't bother about finding a hole," said Dahli. "There are lots of nice little nooks in here."

The mice agreed, and went off to find them without saying thank-you.

Not long after, Dahli heard awful screaming from Carnatia's room.

When she went in, Chrysanthia and Carnatia were standing on the dressing table together.

"Mice!" screamed Carnatia.

"Oh, help! Help!" howled Chrysanthia.

"Oh, dear," said Dahli. "Has it spoiled your nap?"

"Of course it has!" screamed Carnatia.

"Of course it has!" howled Chrysanthia.

Just then the mice went out, carrying their suitcases, and were never seen again.

WHEN IT WAS time for everybody to get dressed, Carnatia and Chrysanthia had a terrible time.

Dahli kept bringing them the wrong shoes, putting on their dresses back to front, and getting things tangled up in their hair. When they told her to tie their sashes in bows, she managed to get the ends tangled up and tied them together.

"Come along," said King Archibald impatiently. "The carriages are waiting. There is some bread and cheese in the kitchen for you, Dahli," he added.

"Thank you," said Dahli. "How I would have liked to have gone to the ball."

"I'm afraid it's quite out of the question," said King Archibald pompously. "For one thing, you have no ball dress to wear."

"I certainly couldn't have borrowed one of your daughters' dresses," agreed Dahli. "They'd be *much* too big for me."

WHEN THEY HAD driven off, Dahli put on her best dress, with only one patch on it, and combed her hair. Then she left the castle and set out to walk to the palace where the ball was being held. The palace stood on a hilltop, and she could see the lights gleaming. Princess Chrysanthia and Princess Carnatia had said that the ball was being given by a handsome prince, and Dahli thought she would like to see just how handsome he was. Luckily, as she was walking along, a baker's cart drove up. The baker was taking cakes to the palace, and he offered Dahli a lift.

When they arrived at the back door, Dahli thanked the baker. She went straight up to the butler and said, "I am the new maid."

The butler was so flustered by all the preparations for the ball that he didn't stop to argue. He simply gave her a big apron, which hid the patch nicely, and a tray of chocolate bonbons, and told her to go up into the ballroom and offer them to the prince's guests.

Dahli did as she was told, very pleased that her plan had worked. She went from guest to guest until she came to a huge crowd of ladies, all fluttering their fans and chattering around somebody wearing a crown.

"Ah," thought Dahli. "This must be the prince."

So she edged in between all the ladies, curtsied, and held up the tray.

"A chocolate, your highness?"

How disappointed she was. The prince was fat and silly-looking. He grabbed a handful of chocolates and stuffed them into his mouth.

"Perhaps you'd like to keep the tray," said Dahli, and gave it to him. Then she turned around and went and sat on the balcony.

"If this is what happens at a ball," she said aloud, "I'm not surprised I never wanted to come."

"I couldn't agree more," said a voice.

Princess Dahli turned, and there on the seat beside her was a handsome young man with a patch on his sleeve.

"I'm Prince Peregrine," said the young man, "the fat prince's cousin."

"How do you do," said Dahli. And she told him who she was.

"I'm afraid I've been behaving rather badly," said Prince Peregrine. "You see, my parents are very poor, and they sent me up here to live with my uncle, the king, and the fat prince. The fat prince seemed to think I'd make a good servant, but whenever I got things right, he used to shout and throw shoes at me, so today I've been getting everything wrong for a change. He told me to buy him a gold cloak, and I pretended I thought he'd said a gold clock. And when he told me to polish his crown, I polished it with boot polish, and it's gone black, and he's had to borrow one from his father that doesn't fit properly. Also there were some spiders that lived in the attic where I sleep, and I persuaded them to go and spin a big web all over the prince's new clothes."

When Prince Peregrine had finished, Dahli told him what she had done about Chrysanthia and Carnatia, and then she and the prince sat and laughed for nearly ten minutes.

After that, they decided they would go back into the ballroom and dance together.

It was not long before King Archibald noticed.

"How dreadful!" he exclaimed. "There's Dahli in an apron, dancing around right in the middle of the floor."

Carnatia and Chrysanthia, who had both been trying to

dance with the fat prince at the same time, screamed with anger. The fat prince went and told his father, the king.

"How unpleasant!" muttered the fat prince's father. "We can't have Peregrine dancing about at your ball, looking so ragged. Besides, he's twenty times better-looking than you are, and people might notice. Go and tell him I'll give him a castle and some lands if he'll promise to leave at once."

King Archibald had just sent his page down to Dahli.

"King Archibald," said the page, "says he will give you a wardrobe full of dresses, and a casket full of pearls, if you will go home and stop showing him up in front of all these people, in that apron."

"Done!" said Dahli to the page.

"Done!" said Peregrine to the fat prince.

"A whole castle will be a bit big for just my parents and me," remarked Prince Peregrine to Dahli as they were leaving. "Perhaps you and your parents would like to come and stay."

"We'd love to," said Dahli.

PRINCESS DAHLI'S MOTHER and father and Prince Peregrine's mother and father got along very well, and when Dahli and Peregrine got married, everyone was very pleased.

The only people who weren't pleased were a family of mice who had moved into one of the castle attics. Whenever there was a party downstairs, which there often was, they banged on the floor.

But nobody ever took any notice.

Molly Mullett

PATRICIA COOMBS

nce upon a time, miles and years from here, lived Molly Mullett. She liked to climb trees and run races and jump over things.

Molly lived in a house with her mother and father. The house was in a village. It was a small village but it had a big problem. The big problem was a very large Ogre.

The Ogre was greedy and troublesome. Only the night before, he had taken all the corn and pigs and gold he could carry. It was the second time in a month that he had robbed the village. He had also stolen some of the king's horses. Soon there would be no food or gold at all left in the village, and winter was coming.

In the Mullett house Molly took her father his slippers.

Mr. Mullett wanted a son. Whenever he looked at Molly he said, "I do not need a sneezley, wheezley, sniveling girl. If I had a son like me, he would make short work of that Ogre. He would be famous. And the village would be saved."

"I am not sneezley and wheezley and I do not snivel," said Molly.

Mr. Mullett whacked Molly for talking back.

"I always tell the truth," said Molly, "even when it hurts."

Out in the kitchen, Mrs. Mullett sighed. Mr. Mullett went back to his snoring.

Mrs. Mullett was always sweeping and weeping, cooking and looking, washing and wishing, frying and sighing, sitting and knitting.

Molly went to help Mrs. Mullett. Together they hung the wash. In the fields around them the crops were mashed and smashed by the Ogre's boots. Carts and wagons were overturned.

Molly took off her apron. "Mrs. Mullett," said Molly. "It is time for me to have an adventure. I have had enough of sweeping and weeping, frying and sighing, washing and wishing, cooking and looking."

"I don't think you should . . ." said Mrs. Mullett.

"Why?" asked Molly.

"I can't think why," said Mrs. Mullett, "but I'm sure . . ."

"Someone must take care of that Ogre," said Molly. "And no one else is doing it. So I will. The king has offered a reward. I will bring it home for you and Mr. Mullett. Mr.

Mullett will see, once and for all, that I am not a wheezley, sneezley, sniveling person."

Mrs. Mullett fixed a bundle for Molly to take. She was still cooking, and looking out the window as Molly went away.

Molly walked and walked until she came to the king's castle. She said to the guard at the door, "I have come to see the king."

Molly waited and waited. At last she got to see the king.

"That troublesome Ogre has taken nearly all our food and gold," said Molly. "I am going to get it back. I may need some help getting across . . ."

"Haw!" said the king. "You are a mere girl. A wheezley, measley, sneezley girl! Ten of my best soldiers have already been thrown back across Black Gulch by the Ogre. He smashed the bridge and gave them sprains and bruises and broken bones. He toasted and roasted their horses, saddles and all, and ate them for lunch. Go home. Stay indoors. The queen does a lot of sewing. You ought to try it."

"If you won't help me, I'll do it myself," said Molly. Out of the castle she marched and down the road.

Molly walked and walked and walked. It began to get dark. At last Molly came to bottomless Black Gulch. It was a long way across the gulch. But she could see a reddish glow and black smelly clouds from the Ogre's kitchen on the other side.

Molly sat on a stone to think. She opened her bundle to get something to eat while she thought.

As soon as she touched the bundle, a blackbird flew out of the shadows and landed beside her. Molly shared her sandwich with the blackbird.

"There must be a way I can get across," said Molly.

The blackbird pecked at something in the bottom of her bundle.

"A ball of yarn!" said Molly. "Whatever am I to do with that?"

The blackbird tugged at Molly's braid. Molly grinned. "A braid for a bridge!" Molly took the yarn and braided and braided and braided until she had a strip as long and as strong as a rope.

The blackbird took one end in his beak. He flew into the darkness over Black Gulch. When it was all unwound, there was a tug at the other end. The blackbird flew back to Molly. Molly bent down and tied the yarn around a big stone.

Molly looked at the braid stretching across Black Gulch. "A bridge," said Molly, "but it will never hold me!"

The blackbird bobbed his head. He flew to the bridge. He hopped out on it. Molly tried it with one foot. Then the other. It seemed as wide as a path, and with a grin she ran across Black Gulch. The blackbird flew beside her.

The glow from the Ogre's kitchen lit up the jagged rocks and scorched trees. Molly crept closer and closer. She looked in the window.

The Ogre was asleep in his chair. Dozens of plates and bowls and pots and pans were piled around him. The Ogre's

wife was washing and drying stacks and stacks of dishes. A smaller Ogre was sitting on the floor. He was sniveling and driveling and bawling and squalling.

In one corner the stolen gold was heaped up and spilling from the sacks.

The blackbird tapped softly at the window. Molly pushed it open. The blackbird flew in. He flew at the small Ogre and gave him a pinch.

The small Ogre screamed so loudly that the Ogre woke up with an angry roar.

"I'm sorry, dear," said the Ogre's wife. She picked up the smaller Ogre and took him off to bed.

The Ogre stomped around the kitchen. He picked up two pies and a cake and ate them in three gulps. He was about to eat another pie, when the blackbird landed on it. The Ogre made a grab for the bird. The bird flew to a corner. With a roar the Ogre chased the blackbird around and around and around. There were so many dishes and pots and pans on the floor that the Ogre stumbled. One foot got stuck in a pot and the Ogre went sprawling.

Molly saw her chance. She slipped through the window and raced to the corner where the sacks of gold were piled.

"It's a good thing I'm strong," said Molly. She heaved a sack of gold over her shoulder. Just as she got to the window the Ogre sat up. He saw her. Out the window went Molly with the sack of gold, the blackbird right behind her.

Into the darkness they went, back toward Black Gulch. The Ogre came roaring after them. The iron pot sounded

like thunder as the Ogre came stumbling over the rocks. Molly was quick as well as strong. She zigged and she zagged and she ducked and dodged, and the iron pot slowed the Ogre down enough for Molly to keep ahead, just out of reach.

Molly got to the bridge. She raced across. Behind her, the blackbird flew at the Ogre's head. He pecked at his ears and tweaked his beard. By the time the Ogre got to the gulch, Molly was on the other side. The blackbird flew back to Molly, the yarn in his beak. She rolled up the yarn and hid it under a stone. The blackbird showed her the way home in the dark.

Behind them they could hear the Ogre rumbling and grumbling and roaring, the iron pot banging over the stones.

"Well done, blackbird," said Molly. "Thank you." She took a cookie from her bundle and crumbled it in her hand for him to eat.

By the time the moon went down, Molly was home and asleep in her bed, the sack of gold beside her. The blackbird had flown away.

In the morning Molly showed Mrs. Mullett and Mr. Mullett the gold.

"I got it back from the Ogre last night," said Molly.

Mr. Mullett rubbed his eyes and blinked.

"Now I will take it to the king," said Molly. "We will get a reward and the village will have some gold to buy food."

"Wait," said Mr. Mullett. He put on his best clothes. He shaved. He took the sack of gold and he and Molly went to see the king.

The king beamed. "Thank you, Mullett," said the king. "You have done what ten of my best soldiers could not do. You are strong and brave."

"Oh, no, King, sir," said Mr. Mullett. "Molly here, she was the one."

"Ah, Mullett," cried the king, "you are as gallant as you are brave."

"But Molly, she—" said Mr. Mullett.

"Foolishness! Nonsense! Haw!" cried the king. "A mere girl, a measley, wheezley, sneezley girl outwit the Ogre! Haw!"

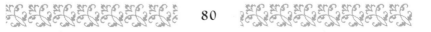

And the king gave Mr. Mullett the reward and said, "The whole kingdom thanks you, Mullett, for your courage and bravery."

Mr. Mullett turned very red and mumbled, "Thank you, King, sir."

Molly shrugged and grinned. She knew the truth, even if the king didn't. And it was her adventure, not Mr. Mullett's, or the king's, or anybody else's.

Meanwhile, the Ogre had gotten his foot out of the cooking pot and he was angry. One night, back he came across Black Gulch, swinging his sword and roaring. He squashed houses and barns, smashed the rest of the fields into mud, and knocked down part of the castle walls.

The king was cross about the castle. He called in the Royal Seer. Then the king went to see Mr. Mullett.

"See here, Mullett," said the king. "You'll have to get rid of the Ogre altogether. Getting the gold back is not enough. The Royal Seer thinks it is the Ogre's sword that gives him his great strength. Without the sword he is merely a roaring, boring oaf. He very likely keeps the sword under his pillow while he sleeps. All you have to do is get the sword away from him. Then he won't bother us anymore."

"ME? The Ogre's *sword?*" Mr. Mullett choked on his pipe. "I can't do that! That's very dangerous and—"

"Haw! Nonsense, my good fellow! You're too modest. I am *ordering* you to do it. If you aren't at the castle tomorrow with the sword, Mullett, it's the dungeon for you."

The king rode away. Mr. Mullett went to lie down and rest. He did not feel very well.

"Mrs. Mullett," said Molly, "it is time for another adventure."

Mrs. Mullett fixed Molly a bundle to take with her. Still cooking and looking, she watched Molly walking down the path.

By the time it began to get dark, Molly was climbing among the rocks at the edge of Black Gulch. She found where she'd hidden the yarn. As soon as she touched it, the blackbird flew from the shadows and landed beside her. Molly sat down and opened her bundle. She shared her sandwich with the blackbird.

"This is an even bigger adventure than the first," said Molly. "I'm glad I'm not afraid of being scared. Mr. Mullett would be most unhappy if the king put him in a dungeon."

They finished eating and the blackbird pecked at something in the bottom of the bundle. Molly looked. It was a small pair of scissors.

"What shall I do with these against the Ogre's sword?" said Molly.

The blackbird pecked at her pocket. Molly grinned and shrugged. She put the scissors in her pocket. As he had before, the blackbird took the braided yarn in his beak and flew over Black Gulch and back again to Molly.

Molly ran quickly across the strip of bridge. The glow from the Ogre's kitchen shone bright as a red angry moon.

Molly looked in the window. The Ogre's wife was just

taking the screaming small Ogre off to bed. The Ogre was in his chair, smoking a cigar and drinking from a barrel of the king's best brandy.

The blackbird tapped at the window. Molly opened it. The blackbird flew inside. He tweaked the Ogre's hair. The Ogre roared and leaped to his feet.

The blackbird pinched the Ogre's ears until they bled. The Ogre grabbed for him. Around and around and around they went, the Ogre roaring and reaching. Around the kitchen and down the hall they went.

Molly saw her chance. Quick as a minnow, she slipped inside and hid herself among the sacks of gold.

Seconds later the Ogre came howling and scowling back again. He swung his sword at the blackbird and chopped off a few tail feathers just as the blackbird flew out the window. The Ogre slammed the window shut.

"Dratted bird," growled the Ogre. He stomped over and had a few blackbird pies and two gallons of pig stew for a snack.

The Ogre's wife trudged back to the kitchen to wash more dishes and pots and pans. As she reached for a towel, she screeched: "EEEE! A mouse! A mouse!"

"Where?" roared the Ogre.

"There!" The Ogre's wife pointed to where Molly was hidden among the sacks of gold.

Before Molly could think or blink, the Ogre's hand lifted her into the air.

"Well, well, a village mouse! A gold-stealing mouse

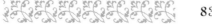

come back for more. A measley, sneezley, wheezley mouse, ah-ha! oh-ho! ho-ha!" laughed the Ogre with his terrible smelly laugh.

"Quick, a sack for this mouse, wife! Tomorrow I will fix it a cage and it will be a pet for our Ogrelet. We can watch him squeeze and pinch it!"

The Ogre stuffed Molly into a sack and tied a big knot at the top. He dropped it at his feet and yawned.

"I'll sleep well tonight," roared the Ogre. He patted his belly and belched his terrible belch. Off to bed went the Ogre and his wife. Before long their huge snores shook the walls and rattled the pots and pans.

Molly fought to get out of the sack. She kicked and pushed and shoved with all her might. No matter how hard she tried, the knot held fast. Molly stopped kicking.

"I just have to think my way out of this," Molly said to herself. Then she remembered. "The scissors! I forgot about the scissors!"

Molly took the scissors out of her pocket. With a snippety-snip-snick she cut a hole in the sack and slipped out. She ran to the window and opened it for the black-bird.

With the blackbird on her shoulder, she tiptoed down the long, long dark hall to the Ogre's room.

The Ogre's snores were deafening. And they smelled terrible. Molly crept up beside the Ogre's bed. A gleam of moonlight shone on the handle of the sword sticking out from under the Ogre's pillow.

Molly grabbed the handle of the sword. She pulled it from under the pillow and the Ogre's snoring head.

In a flash Molly was out of the room, down the hall, across the kitchen and out the window, the blackbird right beside her. Between the rocks and trees they ran. They had not gone far when there was a terrible roar behind them. The Ogre, awakened by his own snores, had found his sword gone and the sack empty.

Molly ran faster than she'd ever run before. She and the blackbird were over the bridge and had it rolled up as the Ogre got to the gulch. The Ogre roared and howled and yowled. All at once there were other sounds. The sounds of trees being pulled up by the roots and thrown across the gulch.

"I think the Royal Seer was wrong about the Ogre's sword," said Molly. "He's making a bridge! He's as strong as ever, and here he comes!"

The Ogre strode across. Molly swung the Ogre's sword at the Ogre's shins. He howled a terrible howl. The sword was very sharp and Molly's aim was very good.

Another swing of the sword and the Ogre lost his balance. Down, down, down into bottomless Black Gulch tumbled the Ogre. Rocks and trees tumbled down with him.

The sound of hooves came from the darkness behind Molly. The king and his soldiers, hearing roars and crashes and sounds of battle, had come to help.

The king got down from his horse. "Where's Mullett?" he cried. "Dear me, the Ogre must have swallowed him before he fell into the gulch."

"Nonsense," said Molly, "I'm the only Mullett here." She leaned on the Ogre's sword to catch her breath. "Mr. Mullett has no taste for adventure. Doubtless he is in bed, dreaming of breakfast."

The Ogre's roars echoed from deep in the gulch, then faded to silence.

The king knelt at Molly's feet. "You have saved us all from the Ogre's power. You are the strongest and bravest person in the kingdom. Whatever you want that I can grant, you shall have."

Molly shrugged and grinned and thanked the king. "I just want to have adventures. I can find them myself, with the blackbird's help."

The king knighted Molly then and there. He rode her home on his Royal Horse, the blackbird on her shoulder. On the way, Molly told the king the tale of her adventures with the blackbird and the Ogre.

"Henceforth," said the king, "the blackbird will be the Royal Bird of our kingdom, and you, Molly Mullett, will be our Very Most Royal Knight."

The king rode up to the door of Molly's house and helped her down from the horse.

Mr. Mullett crawled out of bed and peered out the door. "The king is here! Tell him I'm sick!"

"Molly's home," said Mrs. Mullett. "And she has the Ogre's sword."

The next day everyone in the village helped build a bridge across Black Gulch. Then they took their carts and baskets and wagons and brought back everything the Ogre had stolen from them. Everything he hadn't eaten. The Ogre's wife and the small Ogre had run far away.

Not long after that, Mrs. Mullett had a son. Mr. Mullett made a great fuss over him. "At last, all my dreams will come true!" said Mr. Mullett.

When the baby cried, Mr. Mullett waved the Ogre's sword and told him to be brave. The baby yelled louder.

Molly shrugged and grinned and picked up the baby. "Mr. Mullett," she said, "I do not think you'll ever learn."

Mr. Mullett didn't whack her. He sighed. Molly always told the truth, when it hurt and when it didn't.

"Mrs. Mullett," said Molly, "why did you put the ball of yarn and the scissors into my bundle?"

Mrs. Mullett sat quietly sewing and knowing. She simply smiled.

Molly gave her a kiss and put down the baby. Then she went to play baseball with the king and the other knights.

Gudgekin the Thistle Girl

JOHN GARDNER

 n a certain kingdom there lived a poor little thistle girl. What thistle girls did for a living—that is, what people did with thistles—is no longer known, but whatever the reason that people gathered thistles, she was one of those who did it. All day long, from well before sunrise until long after sunset, she wandered the countryside, gathering thistles, pricking her fingers to the bone, piling the thistles into her enormous thistle sack, and carrying them back to her stepmother. It was a bitter life, but she always made the best of it and never felt the least bit sorry for herself, only for the miseries of others. The girl's name was Gudgekin.

Alas! The stepmother was never satisfied. She was arro-

gant and fiercely competitive, and when she laid out her thistles in her market stall, she would rather be dead than suffer
the humiliation of seeing that some other stall had more thistles than she had. No one ever did, but the fear preyed on
her, and no matter how many sacks of thistles poor
Gudgekin gathered, there were never enough to give the stepmother comfort. "You don't earn your keep," the stepmother
would say, crossing her arms and closing them together like
scissors. "If you don't bring more thistles tomorrow, it's away
you must go to the Children's Home and good riddance!"

Poor Gudgekin. Every day she brought more than yes-
terday, but every night the same. "If you don't bring more
thistles tomorrow, it's away to the Home with you." She
worked feverishly, frantically, smiling through her tears, seiz-
ing the thistles by whichever end came first, but never to her
stepmother's satisfaction. Thus she lived out her miserable
childhood, blinded by burning tears and pink with thistle
pricks, but viewing her existence in the best light possible.
As she grew older she grew more and more beautiful, partly
because she was always smiling and refused to pout, whatever the provocation; and soon she was as lovely as any
princess.

One day her bad luck changed to good. As she was jerk-
ing a thistle from between two rocks, a small voice cried,
"Stop! You're murdering my children!"

"I beg your pardon?" said the thistle girl. When she
bent down she saw a beautiful little fairy in a long white and
silver dress, hastily removing her children from their cradle,

which was resting in the very thistle that Gudgekin had been pulling.

"Oh," said Gudgekin in great distress.

The fairy said nothing at first, hurrying back and forth, carrying her children to the safety of the nearest rock. But then at last the fairy looked up and saw that Gudgekin was crying. "Well," she said. "What's this?"

"I'm sorry," said Gudgekin. "I always cry. It's because of the misery of others, primarily. I'm used to it."

"Primarily?" said the fairy, and put her hands on her hips.

"Well," sniffled Gudgekin, "to tell the truth, I do sometimes imagine I'm not as happy as I might be. It's shameful, I know. Everyone's miserable, and it's wrong of me to whimper."

"Everyone?" said the fairy, "—miserable? Sooner or later an opinion like that will make a fool of you!"

"Well, I really don't know," said Gudgekin, somewhat confused. "I've seen very little of the world, I'm afraid."

"I see," said the fairy thoughtfully, lips pursed. "Well, that's a pity, but it's easily fixed. Since you've spared my children and taken pity on my lot, I think I should do you a good turn."

She struck the rock three times with a tiny golden straw, and instantly all the thistles for miles around began moving as if by their own volition toward the thistle girl's sack. It was the kingdom of fairies, and the beautiful fairy with whom Gudgekin had made friends was none other than the fairies' queen. Soon the fairies had gathered all the thistles for a mile around, and had filled the sack that Gudgekin had brought, and had also filled forty-three more, which they'd fashioned on the spot out of gossamer.

"Now," said the queen, "it's time that you saw the world."

Immediately the fairies set to work all together and built a beautiful chariot as light as the wind, all transparent gossamer woven like fine thread. The chariot was so light that it needed no horses but flew along over the ground by itself, except when it was anchored with a stone. Next they made the thistle girl a gown of woven gossamer so lovely that not even the queen of the kingdom had anything to rival it; indeed, no one anywhere in the world had such a gown or has ever had, even to this day. For Gudgekin's head the fairies fashioned a flowing veil as light and silvery as the lightest, most silvery of clouds, and they sprinkled both the veil and the gown with dew so they glittered as if with costly jewels.

Then, to a tinny little trumpeting noise, the queen of the fairies stepped into the chariot and graciously held out her tiny hand to the thistle girl.

No sooner was Gudgekin seated beside the queen than the chariot lifted into the air lightly, like a swift little boat, and skimmed the tops of the fields and flew away to the capital.

When they came to the city, little Gudgekin could scarcely believe her eyes. But there was no time to look at the curious shops or watch the happy promenading of the wealthy. They were going to the palace, the fairy queen said, and soon the chariot had arrived there.

It was the day of the kingdom's royal ball, and the chariot was just in time. "I'll wait here," said the kindly queen of the fairies. "You run along and enjoy yourself, my dear."

Happy Gudgekin! Everyone was awed by her lovely gown and veil; and even the fact that the fairies had neglected to make shoes for her feet, since they themselves wore none, turned out to be to Gudgekin's advantage. Barefoot dancing immediately became all the rage at court, and people who'd been wearing fine shoes for years slipped over to the window and slyly tossed them out, not to be outdone by a stranger. The thistle girl danced with the prince himself, and he was charmed more than words can tell. His smile seemed all openness and innocence, yet Gudgekin had a feeling he was watching her like a hawk. He had a reputation throughout the nine kingdoms for subtlety and shrewdness.

When it was time to take the thistle sacks back to her cruel stepmother, Gudgekin slipped out, unnoticed by anyone, and away she rode in the chariot.

"Well, how was it?" asked the queen of the fairies happily.

"Wonderful! Wonderful!" Gudgekin replied. "Except I couldn't help but notice how gloomy people were, despite their merry chatter. How sadly they frown when they look into their mirrors, fixing their make-up. Some of them frown because their feet hurt, I suppose; some of them perhaps because they're jealous of someone; and some of them perhaps because they've lost their youthful beauty. I could have wept for them!"

The queen of the fairies frowned pensively. "You're a good-hearted child, that's clear," she said, and fell silent.

They reached the field, and the thistle girl, assisted by a thousand fairies, carried her forty-four sacks to her wicked stepmother. The stepmother was amazed to see so many thistle sacks, especially since some of them seemed to be coming to the door all by themselves. Nevertheless, she said—for her fear of humiliation so drove her that she was never satisfied—"A paltry forty-four, Gudgekin! If you don't bring more thistles tomorrow, it's away to the Home with you!"

Little Gudgekin bowed humbly, sighed with resignation, forced to her lips a happy smile, ate her bread crusts, and climbed up the ladder to her bed of straw.

The next morning when she got to the field, she found eighty-eight thistle sacks stuffed full and waiting. The gossamer chariot was standing at anchor, and the gossamer gown and veil were laid out on a rock, gleaming in the sun.

"Today," said the queen of the fairies, "we're going on a hunt."

They stepped into the chariot and flew off light as moonbeams to the royal park, and there, sure enough, were huntsmen waiting, and huntswomen beside them, all dressed in black riding-pants and riding-skirts and bright red jackets. The fairies made the thistle girl a gossamer horse that would sail wherever the wind might blow, and the people all said she was the most beautiful maiden in the kingdom, possibly an elf queen. Then the French horns and bugles blew, and the huntsmen were off. Light as a feather went the thistle girl, and the prince was so entranced, he was beside himself, though he watched her, for all that, with what seemed to her a crafty smile. All too soon came the time to carry the thistle sacks home, and the thistle girl slipped from the crowd unnoticed, and rode her light horse beside the chariot where the queen of the fairies sat beaming like a mother.

"Well," called the queen of the fairies, "how was it?"

"Wonderful!" cried Gudgekin. "It was truly wonderful! I noticed one thing, though. It's terrible for the fox!"

The queen of the fairies thought about it. "Blood sports," she said thoughtfully, and nodded. After that, all the rest of the way home, she spoke not a word.

When the thistle girl arrived at her stepmother's house, her stepmother threw up her arms in amazement at the sight of those eighty-eight thistle-filled sacks. Nonetheless, she said as sternly as possible, "Eighty-eight! Why not a hundred? If you don't bring in more sacks tomorrow, it's the Home for you for sure!"

Gudgekin sighed, ate her dry crusts, forced a smile to her lips, and climbed the ladder.

The next day was a Sunday, but Gudgekin the thistle girl had to work just the same, for her stepmother's evil disposition knew no bounds. When she got to the field, there stood two times eighty-eight thistle sacks, stuffed to the tops and waiting. "*That* ought to fix her," said the queen of the fairies merrily. "Jump into your dress."

"Where are we going?" asked Gudgekin, as happy as could be.

"Why, to church, of course!" said the queen of the fairies. "After church we go to the royal picnic, and then we dance on the bank of the river until twilight."

"Wonderful!" said the thistle girl, and away they flew.

The singing in church was thrilling, and the sermon filled her heart with such kindly feelings toward her friends and neighbors that she felt close to dissolving in tears. The picnic was the sunniest in the history of the kingdom, and the dancing beside the river was delightful beyond words. Throughout it all the prince was beside himself with pleasure, never removing his eyes from Gudgekin, for he thought her the loveliest maiden he'd met in his life. For all his shrewdness, for all his aloofness and princely self-respect, when he danced with Gudgekin in her bejeweled gown of gossamer, it was all he could do to keep himself from asking her to marry him on the spot. He asked instead, "Beautiful stranger, permit me to ask you your name."

"It's Gudgekin," she said, smiling shyly and glancing at his eyes.

He didn't believe her.

"Really," she said, "it's Gudgekin." Only now did it strike her that the name was rather odd.

"Listen," said the prince with a laugh, "I'm *serious.* What is it really?"

"I'm serious too," said Gudgekin, bridling. "It's Gudgekin the Thistle Girl. With the help of the fairies I've been known to collect two times eighty-eight sacks of thistles in a single day."

The prince laughed more merrily than ever at that. "Please," he said, "don't tease me, dear friend! A beautiful maiden like you must have a name like bells on Easter morning, or like songbirds in the meadow, or children's laughing voices on the playground! Tell me now. Tell me the truth. What's your name?"

"Puddin Tane," she said angrily, and ran away weeping to the chariot.

"Well," said the queen of the fairies, "how was it?"

"Horrible," snapped Gudgekin.

"Ah!" said the queen. "Now we're getting there!"

She was gone before the prince was aware that she was leaving, and even if he'd tried to follow her, the gossamer chariot was too fast, for it skimmed along like the wind. Nevertheless, he was resolved to find and marry Gudgekin— he'd realized by now that Gudgekin must indeed be her name. He could easily understand the thistle girl's anger. He'd have felt the same himself, for he was a prince and knew better than anyone what pride was, and the shame of being made to seem a fool. He advertised far and wide for information on Gudgekin the Thistle Girl, and soon the news of the prince's search reached Gudgekin's cruel stepmother in her cottage. She was at once so furious, she could hardly see, for she always wished evil for others and happiness for herself.

"I'll never in this world let him find her," thought the wicked stepmother, and she called in Gudgekin and put a spell on her, for the stepmother was a witch. She made Gudgekin believe that her name was Rosemarie and sent the poor baffled child off to the Children's Home. Then the cruel stepmother changed herself, by salves and charms, into a beautiful young maiden who looked exactly like Gudgekin, and she set off for the palace to meet the prince.

"Gudgekin!" cried the prince, and leaped forward and embraced her. "I've been looking for you everywhere to implore you to forgive me and be my bride!"

"Dearest prince," said the stepmother disguised as Gudgekin, "I'll do so gladly!"

"Then you've forgiven me already, my love?" said the prince. He was surprised, in fact, for it had seemed to him that Gudgekin was a touch more sensitive than that and had more personal pride. He'd thought, in fact, he'd have a devil of a time, considering how he'd hurt her and made a joke of her name. "Then you really forgive me?" asked the prince.

The stepmother looked slightly confused for an instant but quickly smiled as Gudgekin might have smiled and said, "Prince, I forgive you everything!" And so, though the prince felt queer about it, the day of the wedding was set.

A week before the wedding, the prince asked thoughtfully, "Is it true that you can gather, with the help of the fairies, two times eighty-eight thistle sacks all in one day?"

"Haven't I told you so?" asked the stepmother disguised

as Gudgekin, and gave a little laugh. She had a feeling she was in for it.

"You did say that, yes," the prince said, pulling with two fingers at his beard. "I'd surely like to see it!"

"Well," said the stepmother, and curtsied, "I'll come to you tomorrow and you shall see what you shall see."

The next morning she dragged out two times eighty-eight thistle sacks, thinking she could gather in the thistles by black magic. But the magic of the fairies was stronger than any witch's, and since they lived in the thistles, they resisted all her fiercest efforts. When it was late afternoon the stepmother realized she had only one hope: She must get the real Gudgekin from the Children's Home and make her help.

Alas for the wicked stepmother, Gudgekin was no longer an innocent simpleton! As soon as she was changed back from simple Rosemarie, she remembered everything and wouldn't touch a thistle with an iron glove. Neither would she help her stepmother now, on account of all the woman's cruelty before, nor would she do anything under heaven that might be pleasing to the prince, for she considered him cold-hearted and inconsiderate. The stepmother went back to the palace empty-handed, weeping and moaning and making a hundred excuses, but the scales had now fallen from the prince's eyes—his reputation for shrewdness was in fact well founded—and after talking with his friends and advisers, he threw her in the dungeon. In less than a week her life in the dungeon was so miserable, it made her repent and become a good woman, and the prince released her. "Hold your head high," he said, brushing a tear from his eye, for she made him think of Gudgekin. "People may speak of you as someone who's been in prison, but you're a better person now than before." She blessed him and thanked him and went her way.

Then once more he advertised far and wide through the kingdom, begging the real Gudgekin to forgive him and come to the palace.

"Never!" thought Gudgekin bitterly, for the fairy queen had taught her the importance of self-respect, and the prince's offense still rankled.

The prince mused and waited, and he began to feel a little hurt himself. He was a prince, after all, handsome and famous for his subtlety and shrewdness, and she was a mere thistle girl. Yet for all his beloved Gudgekin cared, he might as well have been born in some filthy cattle shed! At last he understood how things were, and the truth amazed him.

Now word went far and wide through the kingdom that the handsome prince had fallen ill for sorrow and was lying in his bed, near death's door. When the queen of the fairies heard the dreadful news, she was dismayed and wept tears of remorse, for it was all, she imagined, her fault. She threw herself down on the ground and began wailing, and all the fairies everywhere began at once to wail with her, rolling on the ground, for it seemed that she would die. And one of them, it happened, was living among the flowerpots in the bedroom of cruel little Gudgekin.

When Gudgekin heard the tiny forlorn voice wailing, she hunted through the flowers and found the fairy and said,

"What in heaven's name is the matter, little friend?"

"Ah, dear Gudgekin," wailed the fairy, "our queen is dying, and if she dies, we will all die of sympathy, and that will be that."

"Oh, you mustn't!" cried Gudgekin, and tears filled her eyes. "Take me to the queen at once, little friend, for she did a favor for me and I see I must return it if I possibly can!"

When they came to the queen of the fairies, the queen said, "Nothing will save me except possibly this, my dear: ride with me one last time in the gossamer chariot for a visit to the prince."

"Never!" said Gudgekin, but seeing the heartbroken looks of the fairies, she instantly relented.

The chariot was brought out from its secret place, and the gossamer horse was hitched to it to give it more dignity, and along they went skimming like wind until they had arrived at the dim and gloomy sickroom. The prince lay on his bed so pale of cheek and so horribly disheveled that Gudgekin didn't know him. If he seemed to her a stranger, it was hardly surprising; he'd lost all signs of his princeliness and lay there with his nightcap on sideways and he even had his shoes on.

"What's this?" whispered Gudgekin. "What's happened to the music and dancing and the smiling courtiers? And where is the prince?"

"Woe is me," said the ghastly white figure on the bed. "I was once that proud, shrewd prince you know, and this is that's become of me. For I hurt the feelings of the beautiful

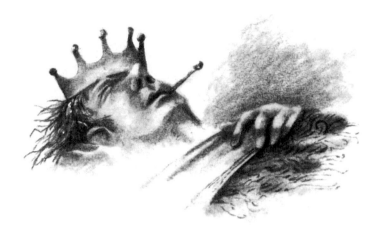

Gudgekin, to whom I've given my heart and who refuses to forgive me for my insult, such is her pride and uncommon self-respect."

"My poor, beloved prince!" cried Gudgekin when she heard this, and burst into a shower of tears. "You have given your heart to a fool, I see now, for I am your Gudgekin, simple-minded as a bird! First I had pity for everyone but myself, and then I had pity for no one but myself, and now I pity all of us in this miserable world, but I see by the whiteness of your cheeks that I've learned too late!" And she fell upon his bosom and wept.

"You give me your love and forgiveness forever and will never take them back?" asked the poor prince feebly, and coughed.

"I do," sobbed Gudgekin, pressing his frail, limp hand in both of hers.

"Cross your heart?" he said.

"Oh, I do, I *do!*"

The prince jumped out of bed with all his wrinkled clothes on and wiped the thick layer of white powder off his face and seized his dearest Gudgekin by the waist and danced around the room with her. The queen of the fairies laughed like silver bells and immediately felt improved. "Why you fox!" she told the prince. All the happy fairies began dancing with the prince and Gudgekin, who waltzed with her mouth open. When she closed it at last it was to pout, profoundly offended.

"Tr-tr-*tricked!*" she spluttered.

"Silly goose," said the prince, and kissed away the pout. "It's true, I've tricked you, I'm not miserable at all. But you've promised to love me and never take it back. My advice to you is, make the best of it!" He snatched a glass of wine from the dresser as he merrily waltzed her past, and cried out gaily, "As for myself, though, I make no bones about it: I intend to watch out for witches and live happily ever after. You must too, my Gudgekin! Cross your heart!"

"Oh, very well," she said finally, and let a little smile out. "It's no worse than the thistles."

And so they did.

The Cat-King's Daughter

LLOYD ALEXANDER

rincess Elena of Ventadorn loved Raimond, Count of Albiclair. However, as much as the two young people had set their hearts on marrying, so King Hugo, father of Elena, had set his against it.

"That lute plucker?" cried Hugo. "That verse scribbler? He should be out hunting, or carousing; or invading the next province, like any self-respecting nobleman. Worse yet, his estates are unspeakably small and his fortune intolerably smaller. In short, the fellow's worthless."

"That's your opinion," said Elena. "Not mine."

"Indeed it is," replied Hugo. "And whose judgment better than the King's?"

"You say that about everything," declared Elena.

"Because pickled herrings happen to give you colic, you've forbidden them to all your subjects. Because holidays bore you, the kingdom has none. You can't abide cats, so you've made it a crime to keep one, to feed one, or even to shelter a kitten."

"So it should be," retorted the King. "Cats! Impudent beasts! They won't fetch or carry. They wave their tails in your face. They stare at you bold as brass, then stick out their tongues and go to washing themselves."

"I call that clean," said Elena, "hardly criminal."

"Worse than criminal, it's disrespectful," snapped the King. "Disobedient and insolent, like headstrong girls who don't take no for an answer."

So, the more Elena urged his consent to marry Raimond, the more stubbornly the King refused. Instead, he sent word for other suitors properly—and profitably—qualified to present themselves at court; and he locked Princess Elena in her chambers, there to receive them and choose one to be her husband.

Princess Elena matched her father in strength of will, and no sooner was the door bolted after her than she determined to escape and make her way to Raimond as quickly as she could. But her chambers in the North Tower of the palace were too high for her to jump from the casement. Since King Hugo disliked ivy, none grew along the steep walls; and, without a handhold, the stones were too smooth for her to clamber down. Though she pulled the sheets and coverlets from her bed and knotted them together, this makeshift ladder barely reached halfway to the courtyard below. The more she cast about for other means, the more clearly she saw there were none. At last, she threw herself on the couch, crying in rage and frustration.

Then she heard a voice say:

"Princess, why do you weep?"

At her feet sat a tabby cat, honey-colored with dark stripes, thin as a mackerel, every rib showing under her bedraggled coat. Though she looked more used to alleys than palaces, she seemed quite at ease amid the soft carpets and embroidered draperies. Instead of crouching fearfully, she studied the Princess with bold curiosity through emerald eyes much the same hue as those of Elena.

"If I had satin cushions to sleep on," said the cat, "and goosedown quilts, and silken bedspreads, I wouldn't be in such a hurry to leave them."

"A cat?" exclaimed the Princess, for a moment forgetting her predicament. "But there are no cats in the palace."

"Well, there is one now," answered the cat, "and my name is Margot." She then explained how she had slipped through the palace gate that morning while the guard was changing.

"But why?" asked Elena. "You must know how my father feels about cats. And here, of all places—"

"Where better?" said Margot. "Who'd expect to find a cat under King Hugo's very nose? I was hoping for a warm cubbyhole to hide in, and a few leftovers from the kitchen. But once inside the palace, I had to dodge so many courtiers, and got so turned around in the hallways and staircases, I was glad for the first open door I came to."

"Poor creature," said Elena, venturing to stroke the cat, "you're hardly more than skin and bones."

"Thanks to your father's decree," said Margot. "Luckily, some people have better sense than to pay it any mind. Now and again, a housewife puts out some scraps or a saucer of milk. For the rest, we forage as best we can. King Hugo hasn't made life easy for a cat."

"Nor a princess," replied Elena, glad for the chance to unburden her heart by telling her troubles to Margot.

After listening attentively to the account, the cat thoughtfully preened her whiskers for several moments, then said:

"We cats won't abide doing what we're forced to do, so I understand your feelings. But I doubt very much you can be made to marry against your will. King Hugo may rant and rave; but, practically speaking, he surely won't tie you hand and foot and drag you by the hair to the wedding ceremony. A bride, kicking and screaming? Hardly flattering for a husband-to-be."

"True," Elena admitted. "But I love Raimond and want him for my husband. How shall I make my father change his mind? What if no one else claimed my hand? I'll make sure they don't! I'll paste a wart on the end of my nose, and paint myself a mustache. That should be discouraging enough."

"Princess," said the cat, "your beauty is too great to hide, no matter what you do."

"I won't eat," said Elena. "I'll starve myself."

"Be sensible," said the cat. "Your father need only wait. Your hunger will soon get the best of you."

"I'm afraid you're right," Elena agreed. "Very well, when these suitors come, I'll refuse to see them. Let them break down the door! I shan't speak a word to them. There's nothing else I can do."

"Yes, there is," said the cat. "What I have in mind might even help us cats as well as you. First, you must do as I ask now. Then, tomorrow, you must stay hidden under the couch. Be warned, however: What happens may bring you joy—or it may break your heart."

Princess Elena could not imagine herself more heartbroken than she was. And so, despite the cat's warning, she willingly agreed. As Margot instructed her, she combed and brushed the cat until the fur was as soft and glistening as her own tresses. Then she draped the cat in one of her silken scarves and tied a necklace of pearls at Margot's waist. She set a diamond bracelet as a crown on Margot's head, and adorned the cat's paws and tail with the finest rings of emeralds, rubies, and sapphires.

Next morning, King Hugo came to order his daughter to make ready for her suitors. But instead of Elena, out of sight beneath the couch, he found Margot, royally attired, comfortably stretched out amid the satin pillows.

"What's this?" roared the King. "What's this cat doing here? Scat! Scat!" He shouted for Elena, but she never stirred. Before the King thought to search the chambers, Margot

glanced calmly at him and, in a voice resembling that of Elena, said:

"Father, how is it that you don't recognize your own daughter?"

At this, King Hugo stared speechless and his head began to whirl. Seeing nothing of Princess Elena in the apartments, he could only believe that she had indeed turned into a cat overnight. Then his bewilderment changed to anger and he shook a finger under Margot's nose:

"You've done it on purpose," he cried, "out of sheer stubbornness, to vex and spite me! How you managed it, I don't know. But I command you: Turn yourself back again! Immediately!"

"That," said Margot, "will be impossible."

King Hugo then declared he would summon the Royal Physician, or, if need be, scour the kingdom for alchemists, astrologers, midwives, village wonder-workers—whoever might transform her once again into human shape.

"That will be of no use," Margot said. "As you see me now, so shall I always be."

"Wretched girl!" King Hugo cried. "Do you mean to make a fool of me? What king ever had a cat for a daughter!"

"What cat ever had a king for a father?" Margot replied.

This only enraged King Hugo the more, and he swore, cat or no, she would receive her suitors and marry the first who was willing.

And so, when the Court Chamberlain came to announce the arrival of Duke Golo de Gobino, the King tried to compose himself and put the best face he could on the matter. For Golo, while hardly the cleverest, was the richest nobleman in the kingdom, with a purse as full as his head was empty. His estates lay beside those of the King; he had a fine regiment of cavalry, excellent stables and kennels, and his marriage to Elena would be all King Hugo ever could wish.

However, when Duke Golo saw the bejeweled Margot, his self-satisfied smile vanished, and he stammered in dismay:

"The Princess? She looks rather like a cat!"

"Pay it no mind," King Hugo said. "She's not quite herself today."

"So I see," replied Golo. "Indeed, I never would have recognized her. Whatever happened?"

"Nothing," said King Hugo. "A trivial indisposition, a minor ailment."

"But, Majesty," quavered Golo, "it may be contagious. Suppose I caught it from her. If I take her for my wife, the same could happen to me."

"In your case," said Margot, "it might be an advantage."

"Come now, Golo," the King insisted, "get on with it. She'll make you a fine wife."

"One thing is certain," added Margot, "you'll never be troubled with mice."

"Majesty," stammered Golo, "I came for your daughter's hand, not her paw."

"Golo!" bellowed the King. "I command you to marry her. Come back here!" But Duke Golo had already darted through the door and was making his way in all haste down the corridor.

King Hugo stormed at the cat for having lost him such a desirable son-in-law. But next came Count Bohamel de Braise, and the King once again tried to put a fair face on bad fortune. Though his estates were not as large as Golo's, Bohamel was a harsh overlord and what he lacked in land he made up in taxing his tenants, and, at this match, King Hugo would have been well satisfied.

However, when Count Bohamel saw Margot, he threw back his head and gave a rasping laugh:

"Majesty, you make sport of me. Some wives have been called cats, but no cat's been called wife. Look at her claws! They'd tear the bedsheets to ribbons. If I ever dared embrace her, she'd scratch me to the bone."

"Your claws are sharper than mine," said Margot. "Ask your tenants."

No matter how King Hugo commanded or cajoled, pleaded or threatened, Bohamel would have no part of marriage with a cat-princess.

"Your misfortune is your own, and not mine," he told the King, and strode from the chamber.

The same happened with the suitors who followed. Each, in turn, found one pretext or another:

"Good heavens, Majesty," protested the Marquis de Cabasson, shuddering. "With a wife like that, I could never invite my friends to dine. She'd never use the proper fork. And what a breach of etiquette when she drank from a saucer."

"I daresay your friends would be too deep in their cups," answered Margot, "to notice what I did with a saucer."

"A cat-wife?" sneered the Seigneur de Malcourir. "She'd dance on the rooftops with every passing tom."

"I assure you," said Margot, "my virtue's greater than yours."

By this time, word had spread through the palace that King Hugo's daughter had become a cat. The councillors and ministers gossiped, the court ladies tittered, the footmen snickered, the kitchen maids giggled, and soon all in the palace were whispering behind their hands or laughing up their sleeves.

"See what you've done!" cried the King. "Shamed me! Humiliated me!"

"How so?" asked Margot. "I'm not ashamed of being a cat. Are you ashamed of being a king?"

King Hugo threw himself down on a chair and held his head in his hands. Not only had his daughter turned into a cat, it was now plain to him she would also turn into a spinster, and instead of a profitable marriage, there would be none at all. He began groaning miserably, blaming his daughter's stubbornness for putting him in such a plight.

That moment, the Court Chamberlain announced the suitors had departed, all but one: Count Raimond.

"How dare he come here?" exclaimed the King. "He's as pigheaded as my daughter—no, no, I don't mean that. Go fetch him, then." He turned to Margot. "Let the fellow see for himself what you've done. You've outwitted yourself this time, my girl. Marry you? One look and he'll change his tune. But at any rate, I'll have seen the last of him."

Alarmed at this, it was all Princess Elena could do to keep silent in her hiding place. She had never expected Raimond to present himself at court, knowing her father would only refuse him. Now she remembered Margot's warning. If Raimond, too, believed her a cat, indeed her heart would break. Margot, sensing her anguish, dangled her tail over the edge of the couch and waved the tip like a cautioning finger.

The Chamberlain ushered in Count Raimond. To Elena, he had never looked handsomer nor had she loved him so much, and she burned to go to him then and there. But, worse than a broken heart was not knowing the strength of his love for her. So, tormented though she was, she bravely held her tongue.

At sight of the cat, Raimond halted. He stood silent a long moment before he said to King Hugo:

"What I heard of Princess Elena I took for idle gossip. Now I see it is true."

With that, he stepped forward and bowed to Margot. Taking her paw in his hand, he said:

"Why, Princess, how well you look today. What a marvelous color your fur is. The stripes set it off to perfection. Your paws are softer than velvet. And what handsome whiskers, fine as threads of silk. You're beautiful as a cat as you were beautiful as a woman."

"What are you saying?" burst out King Hugo. "Have you gone mad? Paying court to a cat?"

"She's still my beloved as much as she's still your daughter," answered Raimond. "Do true lovers part because the hair of one goes white or the back of the other goes bent? Because the cheeks of one may wither, or the eyes of the other may dim? So long as her heart stays unchanged, so shall mine."

"Do you mean to tell me you'd marry her anyway?" cried King Hugo. "You, stand as bridegroom? And I, give her away? She'd make both of us look like fools."

"Majesty," said Raimond, "the only one who can make you look a fool is yourself. Yes, I will marry her if she will have it so. As for you, can it be that you love your daughter less than I love my intended? And yourself more than anyone else?"

At this, King Hugo began blustering and grumbling again. But, after a moment, he hung his head in shame. Finally, he said:

"My daughter is my daughter, whatever ill has befallen her; and I would have helped her least when she needed me the most. Well, Count of Albiclair, you're not the son-in-law I'd have chosen, but the choice was never mine in the first place. Marry, the two of you, if that's what you want. I still don't give a fig for your lute-plucking and verse-scribbling, but I do give you my blessing."

For her part, Elena was overjoyed at these words, and more than ever assured that Raimond was her true love. Again, she was about to leave her hiding place when, to her dismay, she heard Margot reply:

"Alas, there can be no wedding. Our marriage is out of the question."

"What do you mean?" roared King Hugo, now as determined to see his daughter wed Raimond as he had been against it. "You bedeviled me to give my consent. Now you have it."

"By your own decree, cats are against the law," said Margot. "How shall Raimond keep me as a wife when it's forbidden to keep a cat?"

"Blast the decree!" retorted the King. "That's the stupidest thing I ever heard of. I made that law, so I can change it. From this day on, cats are welcome everywhere, even in my palace. In fact, I'll proclaim a new law that all my subjects must obey: Everyone must keep a cat."

"No, Majesty," answered Margot. "Only let cats freely choose their people, and people choose their cats, and we shall get along very well."

At this, Princess Elena sprang from under the couch and threw her arms around the bewildered but joyful Raimond. And King Hugo commanded all the bells to be rung for the betrothal of the two lovers.

Instead of being angry at Margot for having tricked him, King Hugo kept his word, and better. He invited every cat in the kingdom to the wedding and set out for them tables laden with bowls of cream, platters of fish and fowl, and bouquets of catnip. And Margot, as Maid of Honor, carried the bride's train.

King Hugo also repealed his other foolish laws. Though

he grew no fonder of pickled herrings or holidays, he never again forbade them to his subjects. And because he saw to it that all cats were treated with utmost respect, he became known throughout the land as Hugo the Cat-King, a title which hardly pleased him but which he accepted nevertheless.

In gratitude, the Princess would have kept Margot in silks and jewels, but the cat politely declined, saying she was quite comfortable in her own fur. While she stayed with Elena and Raimond happily all their lives, having seen the ways of kings and courtiers, Margot privately judged it far more sensible to be a cat.

The White Seal Maid

JANE YOLEN

On the North Sea Shore there was a fisherman named Merdock who lived all alone. He had neither wife nor child, nor wanted one. At least that was what he told the other men with whom he fished the haaf banks.

But truth was, Merdock was a lonely man, at ease only with the wind and waves. And each evening, when he left his companions, calling out "Fair wind!"—the sailor's leave—he knew they were going back to a warm hearth and a full bed while he went home to none. Secretly he longed for the same comfort.

One day it came to Merdock as if in a dream that he should leave off fishing that day and go down to the sea-ledge and hunt the seal. He had never done such a thing before, thinking it close to murder, for the seal had human eyes and cried with a baby's voice.

Yet though he had never done such a thing, there was such a longing within him that Merdock could not say no to it. And that longing was like a high, sweet singing, a calling. He could not rid his mind of it. So he went.

Down by a gray rock he sat, a long, sharpened stick by his side. He kept his eyes fixed out on the sea, where the white birds sat on the waves like foam.

He waited through sunrise and sunset and through the long, cold night, the singing in his head. Then, when the wind went down a bit, he saw a white seal far out in the sea, coming toward him, the moon riding on its shoulder.

Merdock could scarcely breathe as he watched the seal, so shining and white was its head. It swam swiftly to the sea-ledge, and then with one quick push it was on land.

Merdock rose then in silence, the stick in his hand. He would have thrown it, too. But the white seal gave a sudden shudder and its skin sloughed off. It was a maiden cast in moonlight, with the tide about her feet.

She stepped high out of her skin, and her hair fell sleek and white about her shoulders and hid her breasts.

Merdock fell to his knees behind the rock and would have hidden his eyes, but her cold white beauty was too much for him. He could only stare. And if he made a noise then, she took no notice but turned her face to the sea and opened her arms up to the moon. Then she began to sway and call.

At first Merdock could not hear the words. Then he realized it was the very song he had heard in his head all that day:

> *Come to the edge,*
> *Come down to the ledge*
> *Where the water laps the shore.*
>
> *Come to the strand,*
> *Seals to the sand,*
> *The watery time is o'er.*

When the song was done, she began it again. It was as if the whole beach, the whole cove, the whole world were nothing but that one song.

And as she sang, the water began to fill up with seals. Black seals and gray seals and seals of every kind. They swam to the shore at her call and sloughed off their skins. They were as young as the white seal maid, but none so beautiful in Merdock's eyes. They swayed and turned at her singing, and joined their voices to hers. Faster and faster the seal maidens danced, in circles of twos and threes and fours. Only the white seal maid danced alone, in the center, surrounded by the castoff skins of her twirling sisters.

The moon remained high almost all the night, but at last it went down. At its setting, the seal maids stopped their singing, put on their skins again, one by one, went back into the sea again, one by one, and swam away. But the white seal maid did not go. She waited on the shore until the last of them was out of sight.

Then she turned to the watching man, as if she had always known he was there, hidden behind the gray rock. There was something strange, a kind of pleading, in her eyes.

Merdock read that pleading and thought he understood it. He ran over to where she stood, grabbed up her sealskin, and held it high overhead.

"Now you be mine," he said.

And she had to go with him, that was the way of it. For she was a selchie, one of the seal folk. And the old tales said it: The selchie maid without her skin was no more than a lass.

They were wed within the week, Merdock and the white seal maid, because he wanted it. So she nodded her head at the priest's bidding, though she said not a word.

And Merdock had no complaint of her, his "Sel" as he called her. No complaint except this: she would not go down to the sea. She would not go down by the shore where he had found her or down to the sand to see him in his boat, though often enough she would stare from the cottage door out past the cove's end where the inlet poured out into the great wide sea.

"Will you not walk down by the water's edge with me, Sel?" Merdock would ask each morning. "Or will you not come down to greet me when I return?"

She never answered him, either "Yea" or "Nay." Indeed, if he had not heard her singing that night on the ledge, he would have thought her mute. But she was a good wife, for all that, and did what he required. If she did not smile, she did not weep. She seemed, to Merdock, strangely content.

So Merdock hung the white sealskin up over the door where Sel could see it. He kept it there in case she should want to leave him, to don the skin and go. He could have hidden it or burned it, but he did not. He hoped the sight of it, so near and easy, would keep her with him, would tell her, as he could not, how much he loved her. For he found he did love her, his seal wife. It was that simple. He loved her and did not want her to go, but he would not keep her past her willing it, so he hung the skin up over the door.

And then their sons were born. One a year, born at the

ebbing of the tide. And Sel sang to them, one by one, long, longing, wordless songs that carried the sound of the sea. But to Merdock she said nothing.

Seven sons they were, strong and silent, one born each year. They were born to the sea, born to swim, born to let the tide lap them head and shoulder. And though they had the dark eyes of the seal, and though they had the seal's longing for the sea, they were men and had men's names: James, John, Michael, George, William, Rob, and Tom. They helped their father fish the cove and bring home his catch from the sea.

It was seven years and seven years and seven years again that the seal wife lived with him. The oldest of their sons was just coming to his twenty-first birthday, the youngest barely a man. It was on a gray day, the wind scarcely rising, that the boys all refused to go with Merdock when he called. They gave no reason but "Nay."

"Wife," Merdock called, his voice heavy and gray as the sky. "Wife, whose sons are these? How have you raised them that they say 'Nay' to their father when he calls?" It was ever his custom to talk to Sel as if she returned him words.

To his surprise, Sel turned to him and said, "Go. My sons be staying with me this day." It was the voice of the singer on the beach, musical and low. And the shock was so great that he went at once and did not look back.

He set his boat on the sea, the great boat that usually took several men to row it. He set it out himself and got it out into the cove, put the nets over, and never once heard

when his sons called out to him as he went, "Father, fair wind!"

But after a bit the shock wore thin and he began to think about it. He became angry then, at his sons and at his wife, who had long plagued him with her silence. He pulled in the nets and pulled on the oars and started toward home. "I, too, can say 'Nay' to this sea," he said out loud as he rode the swells in.

The beach was cold and empty. Even the gulls were mute.

"I do not like this," Merdock said. "It smells of a storm."

He beached the boat and walked home. The sky gathered in around him. At the cottage he hesitated but a moment, then pulled savagely on the door. He waited for the warmth to greet him. But the house was as empty and cold as the beach.

Merdock went into the house and stared at the hearth, black and silent. Then, fear riding in his heart, he turned slowly and looked over the door.

The sealskin was gone.

"Sel!" he cried then as he ran from the house, and he named his sons in a great anguished cry as he ran. Down to the sea-ledge he went, calling their names like a prayer: "James, John, Michael, George, William, Rob, Tom!"

But they were gone.

The rocks were gray, as gray as the sky. At the water's edge was a pile of clothes that lay like discarded skins.

Merdock stared out far across the cove and saw a seal herd swimming. Yet not a herd. A white seal and seven strong pups.

"Sel!" he cried again. "James, John, Michael, George, William, Rob, Tom!"

For a moment, the white seal turned her head, then she looked again to the open sea and barked out seven times. The wind carried the faint sounds back to the shore. Merdock heard, as if in a dream, the seven seal names she called. They seemed harsh and jangling to his ear.

Then the whole herd dove. When they came up again they were but eight dots strung along the horizon, lingering for a moment, then disappearing into the blue edge of sea.

Merdock recited the seven seal names to himself. And in that recitation was a song, a litany to the god of the seals. The names were no longer harsh, but right. And he remembered clearly again the moonlit night when the seals had danced upon the sand. Maidens all. Not a man or boy with them. And the white seal turning and choosing him, giving herself to him that he might give the seal people life.

His anger and sadness left him then. He turned once more to look at the sea and pictured his seven strong sons on their way.

He shouted their seal names to the wind. Then he added, under his breath, as if trying out a new tongue, "Fair wind, my sons. Fair wind."

The Dark Princess

RICHARD KENNEDY

here was a child born who was so beautiful that no one could look at her without blinking, and she was a Princess. Each day and each year she became more beautiful. When she was ten, those who spoke to her looked over her shoulder, or turned their heads while speaking. It was as if a great light shone out of her face. When she was a young lady and ready to marry, no one could look into her face at all. The sight would strike them blind. And another thing. The Princess herself was totally blind.

She was not born blind, but became blind year by year as she became more beautiful. The Royal Physician explained the matter to her parents, the King and Queen. He said the condition was caused by a "frontal optical reversal of the cognitive processes acting on the stereoscopic image-blending phenomenon which resulted in a transposed focal plane bilaterally projecting her sight into a dark area of her brain." He could put it more simply than this. "It is like a dark cloud that blocks out the sun. It could pass at any time."

And so, since it could pass at any time, the King and Queen kept her blindness a secret. That was easy enough to do, since it was impossible for anyone to look at the Princess directly, and a great, long-haired dog led her way and guarded her step, and she had the measure of every chair and table in the palace, and every bush and tree in the Royal Garden. Her ear was so clever that she knew the footstep of everyone on tile or on carpet, and their voices, of course. From the rustle of their clothes, she knew what others were wearing, and from the tinkle of metal and the clink of stone, their ornaments and jewelry, and no one could sit so quietly in a room that she would not know he was there.

One day, when the Princess was walking in the garden, the King made a wonderful discovery. He was standing at a stained glass window inside the palace as she passed, and his discovery was that he could look into her face through the dark glass and not be blinded. He called her and spoke to her face to face through the window and was awed by her beauty.

Everyone in the Kingdom who could afford it got himself a piece of colored glass to behold the Princess, and watched her come and go with her dog, her head held in a slight attentive cock, as if she were listening to music they could not hear, or pursuing some fancy in her mind. She carried herself with such aloofness that some thought she was conceited about her great beauty and could not bother to take notice of anyone else. Some said it was only modesty and a sign of good upbringing. But it was neither. She was merely counting her steps and listening to the many sounds that tell the way in total darkness, and feeling the trembling of the leash she held as the dog informed her of a chair or table out of place, a new-dug hole in the garden, a limb across a path, or anything else amiss or strange in her way. The people did not suspect she was blind.

Now this was the state of affairs when the first Prince came to the Kingdom to consider the girl for a bride, and through his glass—yes, even so darkly—she was as beautiful to him as anyone he had ever seen, and he loved her at once. After a while of courtly good manners, they walked in the garden alone, led by the Princess's dog. They stopped by a flowering bush, and the Prince looked at her through his glass and spoke.

"Forgive me," he said, "but this past hour has been an age to me, and there would be nothing left of me but dust if I would wait through a season of wooing to declare myself to you. Let me be plain and quick while I am not yet faded to a shadow by the sight of you. You are more beautiful than anyone I have ever seen or could imagine, and I am helplessly in love with you already."

"Are you?" said the Princess, touching a blossom.

"Forsooth," said the Prince, "my very self with love has leaped from me. I have forgotten who I am, in love. I would not know my face in a mirror. Marry me. Come with me and be my Queen, or say no to me and tell me my name so I may despair over the sound of it forever."

The Princess had been told that the Prince was handsome and well set up, and she had no reason to doubt it. His speech was fair (though a bit extravagant), his manners pleasant, and his voice sounded sweet to her.

"If you love me," said the Princess, "then you may prove it to me."

The Prince dropped to one knee. "Only tell me how," he said. "Any vow, any venture, any danger, any dare..."

"Look at me," said the Princess.

"What?"

"Take away your piece of colored glass and look at me directly."

"But... but..." the Prince stammered, getting to his feet again. "They say that, that if one does..."

"Yes," said the Princess, "if you do, you will be blinded."

"But to be *blind!*" said the Prince. "How awful. Certainly you wouldn't want me to be blind! Sight is more valuable than anything but life itself. How could you love me then?"

"Only then *could* I love you. Then I would believe that you truly loved me, and I would love you."

The Prince protested such an outrageous test of his love, and drew upon arguments from philosophy, law, physics, chemistry, and astronomy to declare the reasons why he could not meet the test. "Give me another test," he demanded.

"There is no other," said the Princess, and plucking a blossom, she turned and walked back to the palace.

The Prince rode away that same day, and the King came to the Princess in her rooms and said, "Did the Prince not please you?"

"He pleased me well enough," she said, brushing the dog with long sweeping strokes, "and I might have loved him."

"But then why did he leave?" asked the King.

"Because he could not love *me*, Father."

"Ye gods, he must have been blind! Excuse me, dear."

"No, he was not blind," said the Princess. "He would have hated that."

And so for a year the princes came, and each in his manner, shy or bold, plain or poetic, declared he had lost his heart in love for the Princess. But none would lose his sight for it, and all of them went away in a silent and puzzled wonder.

Likewise were the King and Queen puzzled. Princes were now coming from very far away, and soon there would be none left at all to come. They wondered—had the princes suspected that the girl was blind? The King and Queen had chosen to keep this a secret, and did not consider it so very unfair since the girl was likely to regain her sight at any moment. And besides, her blindness was a small thing in comparison to her beauty. They simply could not understand. Of course, they did not know of the test the girl proposed. And none could pass that test.

The Princess by this time had satisfied herself that she would not marry, and in these later days she became sad. It was not so much that she was sad because she would not have a husband, for those who do not marry can be happy, but her sadness was in her doubt that there was such a thing as love in the world. So many had told her that they loved her, but none of them would prove it in the way she asked. Then what was this love they spoke about? She was tired of the word.

The Princess walked more slowly than usual now, and sometimes she sat by a window for hours without moving, and she took no delight in stories or music, and if dessert had not been served after supper, she would not have noticed. It is a bad sadness to believe that there is no love in the world, and people have hanged themselves for less gloomy discoveries.

But it was worse yet than that. Believing that there was no love in the world was her lesser sorrow. Her greater sorrow was this: What if a Prince *should* give up his eyesight out of love for her? What had she to give in return? She was already blind. Just one time there was a Prince who had paused thoughtfully when she told him the test, and for a terrible few throbbing moments she feared that this one would actually go blind for her, and a strange agony rose in her breast, and she was relieved when the Prince began his protest.

Later and alone, the poor girl concluded that her fear and agony in those moments was for the reason that even though there may be love in the world, there was no love in herself. She had nothing to give to prove it. That was her greater sorrow. She believed she could not love.

When her thoughts followed along these dismal lines for too long a time, and she found herself wondering how it would feel to fall from the great tower, and how long it would take before she was broken on the ground, the Princess shook her head and hurried to the kitchen to have a picnic packed for herself, and she took herself away from her thoughts of oblivion, out through the garden and beyond the great stone lion gates on the path that went down to the ocean. Her dog led the way, and as the surf grew louder in the distance and the first smell of salt air came to her, she hummed a tune to raise her spirits. Only the sea was large enough to fill the emptiness she sometimes felt inside herself, and there at the edge of the land where a cliff dropped into the crashing surf below, she would eat her picnic lunch and drink a glass of wine, and sometimes she would smile.

On this day there was someone else out on a picnic at that place. The Court Fool was sitting with his legs dangling over the side of the cliff, and next to him was a bottle of wine and some chicken bones. The dog barked, and the Fool turned to look. He blinked, and quickly got out his piece of colored glass and watched the Princess approach. As usual, she seemed to take no notice of him at all, and it was not his place to greet her first. What a strange, distracted girl she seemed to be, and he concluded that she was probably caught up in a daydream. In fact, she came walking out onto the cliff so purposefully and yet so much like a sleepwalker that he was certain she was going to walk right over the edge, and he called, "Look out!"

Hardly were the words out of his mouth, when she stopped.

"Look out?" she said, turning toward him but looking over his head. "Look out for what? I am exactly five steps from the edge of the cliff." She had recognized his voice, of course. "What are you doing out here, Fool?"

"Well, as you see, Princess, I came for a little picnic like yourself. Roast chicken, a little wine. Will the dog eat the bones?"

"You are certainly a fool if you don't know that chicken bones are dangerous for dogs," she said, and she spread out a cloth to set her picnic basket on. The Fool raked the bones over the side and watched them fall into the surf below. He looked at the Princess again through his colored glass, then took a drink of his wine. He had never been so close to her before, and certainly he had never been alone with her. What could he say? He ventured a common subject: "They say another Prince is coming to visit next week, from very far away."

"I have heard that," said the Princess, breaking some bread and putting a piece of cheese in her mouth. "It matters little."

The Fool had intended to follow up on such a conversation, for he was safe and in his place to talk of the visiting princes, their fine dress and horses, and to gossip of neighboring kingdoms, but instead he said, "Why don't you ever laugh at me?"

The Princess stopped chewing. She started to make a stern face at the Fool, but then she shrugged. "I do laugh, now and again." The truth was, of course, that she had never been able to see his funny antics when he entertained at court, and remembered to laugh only sometimes, when the others laughed.

"No, you don't laugh, not really," said the Fool, "and I am a student of laughing. No, you don't laugh, not like the others. And the others laugh when I see them about the hallways and do a face and a little step for them, but you seem to ignore me."

The Princess folded some ham into her bread. "Perhaps you are not such a funny fool as you think you are."

The Fool plucked at the grass and sprinkled it into the wind blowing up past his legs. "I would think my face was funny enough," he said, and they sat and listened to the ocean. "But I *can* make you laugh," said the Fool at last. "Yes, I could make you laugh this very moment if I wanted to."

"I guarantee you cannot," said the Princess, and she smiled. "Stand on your head, stretch out your cheeks and ears, look at me under your legs, and squash your nose. You couldn't make me laugh."

"Then I will, just to show you," said the Fool. "And I will do it with words alone. Be ready to laugh, now, for here it is that will amuse you greatly, and only three words will do it." He took a double gulp of wine and then said, "I love you."

The Princess did not laugh. She lowered her head and gazed very solemnly toward the ground. Presently she said, "Yes, for a Fool to love a Princess—I suppose that might be funny. However, since it isn't true, it isn't funny. Two-score princes have come and gone, and all of them said that they loved me. But none of them did, and you do not, either."

The Princess poured herself a glass of wine and took a sip. "There is no such thing as love, and that's why I don't laugh at you now, and why I rarely laugh. What you think you love you do not, really. I am only beautiful, and if you lost the way to see me, you would not love me."

"No," he said. "It is not your beauty I love, it is *you* I love, it is your *ways* I love. A Fool may look closely to know who a person is, and with little insult, for he need only wag his nose to be excused. And though I have seen you only darkly, I have seen you deeply, and it is you yourself that I love."

Now the Princess did laugh. "Let me tell you something. Will you promise to keep it a secret?"

"In my heart," said the Fool. And so the Princess told him why she had not chosen a Prince to marry, and how she had put her test to them, and how they all had declined to look at her directly and go blind for their love.

"I would be blind for you," said the Fool.

The Princess gathered up her things and put them in the basket. "Then you would be a fool for sure." She folded her picnic cloth and stood up. "Yes, you would be the best fool of all. Any of the princes would have had me for a bride upon looking at me directly. But I cannot marry you, and you would have nothing for it but darkness."

The Fool smiled to himself and nodded. Then he too stood up next to her and looked at her through his colored glass. The Princess could feel the Fool's sadness, and she spoke again before turning to leave.

"You are a good and fortunate fool to believe in love, but your sadness is not as great as it could be. Mine is greater. Remember, I do not believe in love."

"But you *must* believe in love," said the Fool. "I would go blind that you do, for that alone I would go blind."

And then the Princess was reminded of her greater sorrow—her sorrow that even though another might one day give his sight out of love for her, she had nothing to give in return. She shook her head.

"Ah, dear Fool, we could be certain of nothing except that you would be blind. How could I believe? I have nothing to give in return. But here, let me touch your hand before I go."

The Princess reached out her hand, and she felt a thin, smooth object placed in her palm. She caught her breath to cry out, but the Fool cried, "Oh, oh . . ." and she heard him stumble backward, and heard his foot slide on the cliff's edge. He fell without a sound, and she heard him splash in the surf below. She dropped the picnic basket and the piece of colored glass, touched her toe to the edge of the cliff, and leaped into the water to save him, for he was only newly blind.

And there in the darkness below they touched for a moment, and then they drowned.

And in that moment they touched, the sun rose a million times for them, and the Princess and the Fool could see each other and all the things of life and the world more clearly than but a dozen people since the beginning of time. And that moment they touched outlasted the life of the King and Queen, and outlasted the life of the Kingdom. And that moment they touched is lasting still, and will outlast us, too.

Petronella

JAY WILLIAMS

I n the kingdom of Skyclear Mountain, three princes were always born to the king and queen. The oldest prince was always called Michael, the middle prince was always called George, and the youngest was always called Peter. When they were grown, they always went out to seek their fortunes. What happened to the oldest prince and the middle prince no one ever knew. But the youngest prince always rescued a princess, brought her home, and in time ruled over the kingdom. That was the way it had always been. And so far as anyone knew, that was the way it would always be.

Until now.

Now was the time of King Peter the twenty-sixth and

Queen Blossom. An oldest prince was born, and a middle prince. But the youngest prince turned out to be a girl.

"Well," said the king gloomily, "we can't call her Peter. We'll have to call her Petronella. And what's to be done about it, I'm sure I don't know."

There was nothing to be done. The years passed, and the time came for the princes to go out and seek their fortunes. Michael and George said good-bye to the king and queen and mounted their horses. Then out came Petronella. She was dressed in traveling clothes, with her bag packed and a sword by her side.

"If you think," she said, "that I'm going to sit at home, you are mistaken. I'm going to seek my fortune, too."

"Impossible!" said the king.

"What will people say?" cried the queen.

"Look," said Prince Michael, "be reasonable, Pet. Stay home. Sooner or later a prince will turn up here."

Petronella smiled. She was a tall, handsome girl with flaming red hair and when she smiled in that particular way it meant she was trying to keep her temper.

"I'm going with you," she said. "I'll find a prince if I have to rescue one from something myself. And that's that."

The grooms brought out her horse, she said good-bye to her parents, and away she went behind her two brothers.

They traveled into the flatlands below Skyclear Mountain. After many days, they entered a great dark forest. They came to a place where the road divided into three, and there at the fork sat a little wrinkled old man covered with dust and spiderwebs.

Prince Michael said haughtily, "Where do these roads go, old man?"

"The road on the right goes to the city of Gratz," the man replied. "The road in the center goes to the castle of Blitz. The road on the left goes to the house of Albion the enchanter. And that's one."

"What do you mean by 'And that's one'?" asked Prince George.

"I mean," said the old man, "that I am forced to sit on this spot without stirring, and that I must answer one question from each person who passes by. And that's two."

Petronella's kind heart was touched. "Is there anything I can do to help you?" she asked.

The old man sprang to his feet. The dust fell from him in clouds.

"You have already done so," he said. "For that question is the one which releases me. I have sat here for sixty-two years, waiting for someone to ask me that." He snapped his fingers with joy. "In return, I will tell you anything you wish to know."

"Where can I find a prince?" Petronella said promptly.

"There is one in the house of Albion the enchanter," the old man answered.

"Ah," said Petronella, "then that is where I am going."

"In that case I will leave you," said her oldest brother. "For I am going to the castle of Blitz to see if I can find my fortune there."

"Good luck," said Prince George. "For I am going to the city of Gratz. I have a feeling my fortune is there."

They embraced her and rode away.

Petronella looked thoughtfully at the old man, who was combing spiderwebs and dust out of his beard. "May I ask you something else?" she said.

"Of course. Anything."

"Suppose I wanted to rescue that prince from the enchanter. How would I go about it? I haven't any experience in such things, you see."

The old man chewed a piece of his beard. "I do not know everything," he said after a moment. "I know that there are three magical secrets which, if you can get them from him, will help you."

"How can I get them?" asked Petronella.

"Offer to work for him. He will set you three tasks, and if you can do them you may demand a reward for each. You must ask him for a comb for your hair, a mirror to look into, and a ring for your finger."

"And then?"

"I do not know. I only know that when you rescue the prince, you can use these things to escape from the enchanter."

"It doesn't sound easy," sighed Petronella.

"Nothing we really want is easy," said the old man. "Look at me—I have wanted my freedom, and I've had to wait sixty-two years for it."

Petronella said good-bye to him. She mounted her horse and galloped along the third road.

It ended at a low, rambling house with a red roof. It was

a comfortable-looking house, surrounded by gardens and stables and trees heavy with fruit.

On the lawn, in an armchair, sat a handsome young man with his eyes closed and his face turned to the sky.

Petronella tied her horse to the gate and walked across the lawn.

"Is this the house of Albion the enchanter?" she said.

The young man blinked up at her in surprise.

"I think so," he said. "Yes, I'm sure it is."

"And who are you?"

The young man yawned and stretched. "I am Prince Ferdinand of Firebright," he replied. "Would you mind stepping aside? I'm trying to get a suntan and you're standing in the way."

Petronella snorted. "You don't sound like much of a prince," she said.

"That's funny," said the young man, closing his eyes. "That's what my father always says."

At that moment the door of the house opened. Out came a man dressed all in black and silver. He was tall and thin, and his eyes were as black as a cloud full of thunder. Petronella knew at once that he must be the enchanter.

He bowed to her politely. "What can I do for you?"

"I wish to work for you," said Petronella boldly.

Albion nodded. "I cannot refuse you," he said. "But I warn you, it will be dangerous. Tonight I will give you a task. If you do it, I will reward you. If you fail, you must die."

Petronella glanced at the prince and sighed. "If I must, I must," she said. "Very well."

That evening they all had dinner together in the enchanter's cozy kitchen. Then Albion took Petronella out to a stone building and unbolted its door. Inside were seven huge black dogs.

"You must watch my hounds all night," said he.

Petronella went in, and Albion closed and locked the door.

At once the hounds began to snarl and bark. They bared their teeth at her. But Petronella was a real princess. She plucked up her courage. Instead of backing away, she went toward the dogs. She began to speak to them in a quiet voice. They stopped snarling and sniffed at her. She patted their heads.

"I see what it is," she said. "You are lonely here. I will keep you company."

And so all night long, she sat on the floor and talked to the hounds and stroked them. They lay close to her, panting.

In the morning Albion came and let her out. "Ah," said he, "I see that you are brave. If you had run from the dogs, they would have torn you to pieces. Now you may ask for what you want."

"I want a comb for my hair," said Petronella.

The enchanter gave her a comb carved from a piece of black wood.

Prince Ferdinand was sunning himself and working at a crossword puzzle. Petronella said to him in a low voice, "I am doing this for you."

"That's nice," said the prince. "What's 'selfish' in nine letters?"

"You are," snapped Petronella. She went to the enchanter. "I will work for you once more," she said.

That night Albion led her to a stable. Inside were seven huge horses.

"Tonight," he said, "you must watch my steeds."

He went out and locked the door. At once the horses began to rear and neigh. They pawed at her with their iron hoofs.

But Petronella was a real princess. She looked closely at them and saw that their coats were rough and their manes and tails full of burrs.

"I see what it is," she said. "You are hungry and dirty."

She brought them as much hay as they could eat, and began to brush them. All night long she fed them and groomed them, and they stood quietly in their stalls.

In the morning Albion let her out. "You are as kind as you are brave," said he. "If you had run from them, they would have trampled you under their hoofs. What will you have as a reward?"

"I want a mirror to look into," said Petronella.

The enchanter gave her a mirror made of silver.

She looked across the lawn at Prince Ferdinand. He was doing exercises leisurely. He was certainly handsome. She said to the enchanter, "I will work for you once more."

That night Albion led her to a loft above the stables. There, on perches, were seven great hawks.

"Tonight," said he, "you must watch my falcons."

As soon as Petronella was locked in, the hawks began to beat their wings and scream at her.

Petronella laughed. "That is not how birds sing," she said. "Listen."

She began to sing in a sweet voice. The hawks fell silent. All night long she sang to them, and they sat like feathered statues on their perches, listening.

In the morning Albion said, "You are as talented as you are kind and brave. If you had run from them, they would have pecked and clawed you without mercy. What do you want now?"

"I want a ring for my finger," said Petronella.

The enchanter gave her a ring made from a single diamond.

All that day and all that night Petronella slept, for she was very tired. But early the next morning, she crept into

Prince Ferdinand's room. He was sound asleep, wearing purple pajamas.

"Wake up," whispered Petronella. "I am going to rescue you."

Ferdinand awoke and stared sleepily at her. "What time is it?"

"Never mind that," said Petronella. "Come on!"

"But I'm sleepy," Ferdinand objected. "And it's so pleasant here."

Petronella shook her head. "You're not much of a prince," she said grimly. "But you're the best I can do."

She grabbed him by the wrist and dragged him out of bed. She hauled him down the stairs. His horse and hers were in a separate stable, and she saddled them quickly. She gave the prince a shove, and he mounted. She jumped on her own horse, seized the prince's reins, and away they went like the wind.

They had not gone far, when they heard a tremendous thumping. Petronella looked back. A dark cloud rose behind them, and beneath it she saw the enchanter. He was running with great strides, faster than the horses could go.

"What shall we do?" she cried.

"Don't ask me," said Prince Ferdinand grumpily. "I'm all shaken to bits by this fast riding."

Petronella desperately pulled out the comb. "The old man said this would help me!" she said. And because she didn't know what else to do with it, she threw the comb on the ground. At once a forest rose up. The trees were so thick that no one could get between them.

Away went Petronella and the prince. But the enchanter turned himself into an ax and began to chop. Right and left he chopped, slashing, and the trees fell before him.

Soon he was through the wood, and once again Petronella heard his footsteps thumping behind.

She reined in the horses. She took out the mirror and threw it on the ground. At once a wide lake spread out behind them, gray and glittering.

Off they went again. But the enchanter sprang into the water, turning himself into a salmon as he did so. He swam across the lake and leaped out of the water on to the other bank. Petronella heard him coming—*thump! thump!*—behind them again.

This time she threw down the ring. It didn't turn into anything, but lay shining on the ground.

The enchanter came running up. And as he jumped over the ring, it opened wide and then snapped up around him. It held his arms tight to his body, in a magical grip from which he could not escape.

"Well," said Prince Ferdinand, "that's the end of him."

Petronella looked at him in annoyance. Then she looked at the enchanter, held fast in the ring.

"Bother!" she said. "I can't just leave him here. He'll starve to death."

She got off her horse and went up to him. "If I release you," she said, "will you promise to let the prince go free?"

Albion stared at her in astonishment. "Let him go free?" he said. "What are you talking about? I'm glad to get rid of him."

It was Petronella's turn to look surprised. "I don't understand," she said. "Weren't you holding him prisoner?"

"Certainly not," said Albion. "He came to visit me for a weekend. At the end of it, he said, 'It's so pleasant here, do you mind if I stay on for another day or two?' I'm very polite and I said, 'Of course.' He stayed on, and on, and on. I didn't like to be rude to a guest and I couldn't just kick him out. I don't know what I'd have done if you hadn't dragged him away."

"But then—" said Petronella, "but then—why did you come running after him this way?"

"I wasn't chasing him," said the enchanter. "I was chasing *you*. You are just the girl I've been looking for. You are brave and kind and talented, and beautiful as well."

"Oh," said Petronella. "I see."

"Hmm," said she. "How do I get this ring off you?"

"Give me a kiss."

She did so. The ring vanished from around Albion and reappeared on Petronella's finger.

"I don't know what my parents will say when I come home with you instead of a prince," she said.

"Let's go and find out, shall we?" said the enchanter cheerfully.

He mounted one horse and Petronella the other. And off they trotted, side by side, leaving Prince Ferdinand of Firebright to walk home as best he could.

The Wrestling Princess

JUDY CORBALIS

nce upon a time there was a princess who was six feet tall, who liked her own way and who loved to wrestle. Every day, she would challenge the guards at her father's palace to wrestling matches and every day, she won. Then she would pick up the loser and fling him on the ground, but gently, because she had a very kind nature.

The princess had one other unusual hobby. She liked to drive forklift trucks. Because she was a princess, and her father was very rich, she had three forklift trucks of her own—a blue one, a yellow one, and a green-and-purple-striped one with a coronet on each side. Whenever there was a royal parade, the king would ride in front in his golden carriage, behind him would ride a company of soldiers and behind them came the princess driving her striped royal forklift truck. The king got very cross about it but the princess simply said, "If I can't drive my forklift truck, I won't go," and because she was such a good wrestler, the king was too scared to disagree with her.

One day, when the princess had wrestled with sixteen soldiers at once and had beaten them all, the king sent a page to tell her to come to see him in the royal tea-room.

The princess was annoyed.

"Is it urgent?" she asked the page. "I was just greasing the axle of my blue forklift truck."

"I think you should come, Your Highness," said the page respectfully, "His Majesty was in a terrible temper. He's burnt four pieces of toast already and dripped butter all over his second-best ermine robe."

"Oh, gosh," said the princess, "I'd better come right away."

So she got up, picked up her oilcan and went into the royal bathroom to wash her hands for tea. She left oil marks all over the gold taps and the page sent a message to the palace housekeeper to clean them quickly before the king saw them.

The princess went down to the tea-room and knocked loudly on the door. A herald opened it. "The Princess Ermyntrude!" he announced loudly.

"About time, too," said the king. "And where have you been?"

"Greasing the axle of the blue forklift truck," answered the princess politely.

The king put his head in his hands and groaned.

"This can't go on," he sighed tragically. "When *will* you stop messing about with these dirty machines, Ermyntrude? You're nearly sixteen and you need a husband. I must have a successor."

"I'll succeed you, Father," cried the princess cheerfully. "I'd love to be a king."

"You can't be a king," said the king sadly. "It's not allowed."

"Why not?" asked the princess.

"I don't know," said the king. "I don't make the laws. Ask the judges—it's their affair. Anyway, you can't and that's that. You have to have a husband."

He picked up his tapestry and moodily started sewing.

"Ermyntrude," he said after a long silence, "you won't get a husband if you don't change your ways."

"Why ever not?" asked the princess, in surprise.

"To get a husband you must be enchantingly beautiful, dainty and weak," said the king.

"Well, I'm not," said Ermyntrude cheerfully. "I'm nothing to look at, I'm six feet tall and I'm certainly not weak. Why, Father, did you hear, this morning I wrestled with sixteen guards at once and I defeated them all?"

"Ermyntrude!" said the king sternly, as he rethreaded his needle with No. 9 blue tapestry cotton. "Ermyntrude, we are not having any more wrestling and no more forklift trucks either. If you want a husband, you will have to become delicate and frail."

"I *don't* want a husband," said the princess, and she stamped her foot hard. The toast rack wobbled. "*You* want me to have a husband. I just want to go on wrestling and looking after my trucks and driving in parades."

"Well, you can't," said the king. "And that's that. I shall lock up the forklift trucks and instruct the guards that there is to be no more wrestling and we shall have a contest to find you a husband."

The princess was furiously angry.

"Just you wait," she shouted rudely, "I'll ruin your stupid old contest. How dare you lock up my forklift trucks. You're a rotten mean old pig!"

"Ermyntrude," said the king sternly, putting down his tapestry, "you will do as you are told." And he got up and left the royal tea-room.

Princess Ermyntrude was very very angry. She bent the toasting fork in half and stamped on the bread.

"Stupid, stupid, stupid," she said crossly. And she went away to think out a plan.

The first contest to find a prince to marry the Princess Ermyntrude took place next day. The king had beamed a message by satellite to all the neighbouring countries, and helicopters with eligible princes in them were arriving in dozens at the palace heliport.

The princess watched them from the window of her room, where she was sulking.

"Stupid, stupid," she said. "Why, not one of them even pilots his own helicopter."

And she went on sulking.

After lunch, the king sent a messenger to announce that the princess was to dress in her best robes and come to the great hall of the palace.

She put on her golden dress and her fur cape and her small golden crown and her large golden shoes (for she had big feet) and down she went.

At the door of the throne room she stopped to give the herald time to announce her name, then she went in.

Seated inside were seventy-two princes, all seeking her hand in marriage.

The princess looked at them all. They all looked back.

"Sit here, my dear," said the king loudly, and under his breath, he added, "and behave yourself!"

The princess said nothing.

"Good afternoon and welcome to you all," began the king. "We are here today to find a suitable husband for the lovely Princess Ermyntrude, my daughter. The first competition in this contest will be that of height. As you know, the princess is a very tall girl. She cannot have a husband shorter than herself, so you will all line up while the Lord Chamberlain measures you."

The seventy-two princes lined up in six rows and the Lord Chamberlain took out the royal tape measure and began to measure them.

"Why can't I have a shorter husband?" whispered the princess.

"Be quiet. You just can't," said the king.

"Forty-eight princes left in the contest, Your Majesty," cried the Lord Chamberlain.

"Thank you," said the king. "I'm sorry you gentlemen had a wasted journey, but you are welcome at the banquet this evening."

And he bowed very low.

"The second competition," said the king "will be that of disposition. The Princess Ermyntrude has a beautiful disposition, none better, but she does have a slightly hasty temper. She cannot have a husband who cannot match her temper. So we shall have a face-pulling insult-throwing contest. The Lord Chamberlain will call your names one by one and you will come forward and confront the princess, pull the worst face you can manage, put on a temper display and insult her."

"Your Majesty, is this wise? Twenty-four of the princes have retired in confusion already," hissed the Lord Chamberlain.

"Weaklings," murmured the princess sweetly.

The first prince stepped forward. The Princess Ermyntrude pulled a repulsive face and he burst into tears.

"Eliminated," said the Lord Chamberlain running forward with a box of tissues. "Next!"

The next and the next after him and the prince following *them* were all eliminated and it was not until the fifth competitor crossed his eyes, stuck out his tongue and shouted, "Silly cry baby," at the princess, making her so angry that she forgot to shout back, that anyone succeeded at all.

The fifth prince inspired the next four after him, but the princes after that were no match for Princess Ermyntrude until the eighteenth and nineteenth princes called her "Crow face" and "Squiggle bum" and made her giggle.

By the end of the contest, there were seven princes left, all taller and more insulting than the princess.

"And now," said the king, "for the third and final contest. The third competition," he continued, "will be that of strength. As you may know, the Princess Ermyntrude is very strong. She cannot have a weaker husband so you will all line up and wrestle with her."

"Why can't I have a weaker husband?" whispered the princess.

"Be quiet. You just can't," said the king.

So the Lord Chamberlain lined up the seven princes and just as they were being given their instructions, the princess, who was flexing her arm muscles, glanced over at the watching crowd of commoners and noticed a short man covered in helicopter engine oil standing at the back. Because she was so tall, Princess Ermyntrude could see him clearly and, as she looked, he looked back at her and winked quite distinctly. The princess looked again. The short man winked again.

"*Helicopter* engine oil!" thought the princess. "That's the sort of man I like."

Just then the short man looked at her and, forming his mouth carefully, whispered silently, "Choose the seventh. Don't beat him."

The princess felt strangely excited. She looked again. The little man pointed discreetly to the tall, rather nervous-looking prince at the end of the line-up. "That one," he mouthed.

Princess Ermyntrude didn't much like the look of the seventh prince, but she did want to please the helicopter mechanic so she nodded discreetly, rolled up her golden sleeves and stepped forward to take on the first prince.

CRASH! He hit the mat with staggering force.

CRASH, CRASH, CRASH, CRASH, CRASH.

The next five princes followed. The poor seventh prince was looking paler and paler and his knees were beginning to buckle under him. The princess looked quickly at the mechanic, who nodded briefly, then she moved towards the seventh prince. He seized her feebly by the arm.

"Good heavens, I could floor him with one blow," thought the princess, but she didn't. Instead, she let herself go limp and floppy and two seconds later, for the first time in her life, she lay flat on her back on the floor.

The crowd let out a stupendous cheer. The king and the Lord Chamberlain rushed forward and seized the hands of the young prince.

The poor prince looked very pale.

"This is terrible, terrible," he muttered desperately.

"Nonsense," cried the king. "I award you the hand of the princess and half my kingdom."

"But Sire . . ." stammered the prince. "I can't."

"Can't!" shouted the king. "What do you mean, can't. You can and you will or I'll have you beheaded!"

There was a scuffle in the crowd and the helicopter mechanic darted forward and bent low at the king's feet.

"Majesty," he murmured reverently, "Majesty. I am the prince's helicopter pilot, mechanic and aide. Prince Florizel is overcome with shock and gratitude. Is that not so, Sire?" he asked, turning to the prince.

"Um, yes, yes, that's right," said the prince nervously.

The mechanic smiled.

"Prince Florizel, of course, must have the blessing of *his* father, the King of Buzzaramia, whose kingdom adjoins your own, before the ceremony can take place. Is that not so, Sire?"

"Definitely," said the prince.

"Quite, quite," said the king, "I favour these old customs myself. The princess will fly there tomorrow to meet him, in her own royal helicopter."

"And I shall pilot myself," said the princess.

"We shan't go into *that* now," said the king. "Here, you may kiss the princess."

With a small sigh, the prince fainted dead away.

"Shock," said the pilot hastily. "Clearly shock, Your Majesty. It's not every day he wins the hand of such a beautiful, charming and talented young lady."

And he looked deep into the princess's eyes.

The prince was carried out to his helicopter and flown

off by his pilot, with instructions that the Princess Ermyntrude would fly in the following day.

The rest of the contestants and the princess had a large and elegant banquet with a six-metre chocolate cake in the shape of a heart and litres of ice-cream.

"Who made that heart?" asked Ermyntrude.

"I ordered it from Cook," said the king.

"Well, *I* think it's soppy. A heart!" said the princess in disgust.

Next morning she was up early and, dressed in her frog-green flying suit and bright red aviator goggles, she slipped out to her helicopter before the king was up, climbed in and was just warming up the engine, when the Lord Chamberlain came rushing out into the garden.

"Stop, stop," he cried waving his arms wildly. "Stop. His Majesty, your father, is coming too."

The Princess Ermyntrude turned off the master switch and leaned out of the window.

"Well, he'd better hurry and I'm piloting," she said carelessly. "I'll wait three minutes and I'm going if he hasn't come by then."

The Lord Chamberlain rushed into the palace and returned with the king hastily pulling his ermine robe over his nightshirt and replacing his nightcap with a crown.

"You're a dreadful girl, Ermyntrude," he said sadly. "Here I am with a hangover from the chocolate cake and you insist on being selfish."

"I'm *not* selfish," said Ermyntrude. "I'm by far the best

pilot in the palace and it's your own fault you've got a hangover if you will encourage Cook to put rum in the chocolate cake. Anyway, all this was your idea. I'm not marrying that silly prince and I'm flying over to tell him so."

"Ermyntrude," cried the king, scandalized. "How can you do such a thing? I'll be ruined. He won the contest. And besides, you've got to marry someone."

"I haven't and I won't," said the princess firmly and she set the rotor blades in action.

Within an hour, they were flying into the next kingdom and soon they could see the palace shining golden on the highest hilltop.

"Over there," said the king mournfully. "Please change your mind, Ermyntrude."

"Never," said the princess positively. "Never, never, never, never, never."

Below them they could see the landing pad with ostrich feathers and fairy-lights along the strip.

Princess Ermyntrude settled the helicopter gently on the ground, waited for the blades to stop turning and got out.

The prince's mechanic was standing on the tarmac.

"A perfect landing," he cried admiringly.

The Princess Ermyntrude smiled. Just then, an older man in ermine-trimmed pyjamas came running across the grass.

"Florizel, Florizel, what is all this?" he cried.

The mechanic picked up an oilcan from beside his feet.

"Put that down, you ninny," cried the man in ermine

pyjamas. "Don't you know this is a royal princess?"

"You're being ridiculous, Father," said the mechanic. "Of course I know she's a princess. I'm going to marry her."

"*You* are?" cried Princess Ermyntrude's father. "My daughter's not marrying you. She's marrying your prince."

"I am marrying him," said the Princess Ermyntrude.

"She certainly is," said the mechanic. "And in case you're wondering, I *am* Prince Florizel. The other one was an imposter."

"But how?" asked the princess.

"Well," said Prince Florizel, "it was all my father's idea that I should go, so I persuaded my mechanic to change places with me. I thought my father would never find out. Then, when I saw the Princess Ermyntrude, I fell instantly in love with her. She had axle grease on her neck and she was so big and strong. Then I realized it was lucky I'd changed places or you'd have eliminated me on height."

"That's right. You're too short," said the king.

"He's not," said the princess.

"No, I'm not, I'm exactly right and so is she," said Prince Florizel. "Then when I saw her pulling faces and shouting insults and throwing princes to the ground, I knew she was the one person I could fall in love with."

"Really?" asked the princess.

"Truly," said Prince Florizel. "Now, come and see my mechanical digger."

And holding the oilcan in one hand and the princess's hand in the other, he led the way to the machine shed.

The king looked at Prince Florizel's father.

"There's nothing I can do with her once she's made up her mind," he said wearily.

"I have the same trouble with Florizel," said the second king. "I say, would you like an Alka-Seltzer and some breakfast?"

"Would I?" said the princess's father. "I certainly would."

So arm-in-arm they went off together to the palace.

And so Princess Ermyntrude and Prince Florizel were married in tremendous splendour.

The Princess Ermyntrude had a special diamond and gold thread boiler suit made for the wedding and she drove herself to the church in a beautiful bright red forklift truck with *E* in flashing lights on one side and *F* picked out in stars on the other and with garlands of flowers on the forks.

Prince Florizel, who had parachuted in for the wedding, wore an emerald and silver thread shirt with silver lamé trousers and had flowers in his beard. On the steps of the church he reached up on tiptoe to kiss the princess as the television cameras whirred and the people cheered, then they ran down the steps and jumped into the royal forklift and steered away through the excited crowds.

"I'm terribly happy," murmured the prince.

"So am I," said the princess. "I say did you bring the hamburgers and the ketchup?"

"All there in the back," said the prince.

"And I remembered the wedding cake. Look at it," said the princess proudly.

"Good heavens," cried Prince Florizel. "It's magnificent."

For the wedding cake was shaped like a giant oilcan.

"Perfect, don't you think?" murmured the princess.

"Absolutely," said the prince.

And they both lived happily ever after.

The Enchanter's Daughter

ANTONIA BARBER

n the cold white land at the top of the world there once lived an Enchanter and his daughter. So great was the power of the Enchanter that, even amid the frozen wastes, the gardens of his palace were bright with scented flowers and sweet with the music of singing birds. Beyond the walls, green fields and woods and lakes of shining water stretched right to the slopes of the icy and impassable mountains that ringed them around.

Here the Enchanter and his daughter lived alone, for they had no need of servants. Whatever they wanted, whether food or warmth or comfort, the Enchanter had only to pass his hand through the air and everything was as he desired. All his long life he had studied the books of the old magicians and necromancers until he had mastered their arts one by one. But each power once gained, whether to conjure gold out of the earth or music out of the air, left him dissatisfied. For he had no need of the gold, nor time to listen to the music.

The Enchanter would not let his daughter leave the valley. When she asked to see what lay beyond the cold white mountains, he said that traveling would weary her. Instead, he transformed the valley.

First it became a tropical island with beaches of white sand and leaning palms with great feathery leaves. The shining lake became a warm lagoon where the Enchanter's daughter swam in the blue water and chased the brightly colored fish through caves of coral.

When she grew tired of this, the Enchanter turned the palace into a castle on a high crag amid pine forests where the deer roamed and the great eagles soared overhead. Watching them, his daughter began to long for freedom.

Then the Enchanter filled the valley with jungle forests where brilliant snakes and butterflies shone like jewels in the green shadows, and tribes of chattering monkeys swung through the treetops for his daughter's amusement. Watching them as they played, she began to long for company.

The Enchanter's daughter was very beautiful. Her hair was black and flowed over her shoulders like a shining waterfall; her eyes were wide and dark like the eyes of a fawn in the forest; her skin glowed like sunlight upon a ripe nectarine. She did not know that she was beautiful, for she saw no one with whom to compare herself. The Enchanter knew, but he had come to take perfection for granted: so he did not praise her and she did not grow vain. Her beauty shone out from all the myriad mirrors on the palace walls, but she passed by with never a glance at them.

The Enchanter called her "Daughter" and did not give her a name. She did not think this strange, for she called him "Father" and she knew no one else. Sometimes in her dreams it seemed to her that she had once had another name, but when she awoke she could not remember it. At other times she dreamed that she was a small flying bird and did not have a name at all.

Having no one but her father, she went in search of him to the high tower where he pored over his books. But he who had once delighted in her company had now no time to talk to her. For having gained by his magic all that life could offer, he found that he was growing old. He saw that age and death would rob him of all his power and possessions unless he could unlock the one secret that had defeated all other sorcerers before him: the secret of eternal youth.

"Do not trouble me, Daughter," he said, turning the pages of a great dusty book, "for unless I unravel this last mystery I am lost."

The Enchanter's daughter saw that her father laid great store by the books. She reached to take one down to look at it more closely. Then for the first time he turned on her in anger, forbidding her to touch the books in which his power and knowledge lay.

"Then give me books of my own," she begged, "for I have no companions and time lies heavy upon my hands."

The Enchanter's mind was on matters of life and death. He raised one hand and waved it distractedly. "You will find storybooks in your room," he said.

His daughter ran down all the stairs of the tower and found to her delight that the floor of her room was piled high with books. They were bound in bright leathers, tooled and edged with gold, and decorated with glowing pictures— for nothing the Enchanter did was ever done by half.

Then for a long time she did not trouble her father again. For she discovered in the books new worlds of which she had never dreamed. She read adventure stories and fairy stories, tales of heroism and tales of romance. She read of happiness and sadness, pain and courage, hope and despair, friendship and love. She learned that there were many lands beyond the mountains and that they were all full of people. She found that there were mothers as well as fathers—and brothers and sisters, cousins and friends. And all the people in the books had names, which made her wonder again about the name in her dreams she could never quite remember.

Then the Enchanter's daughter went once more to her father, who could scarcely be seen amid piles of musty volumes.

"Father," she asked him, "what is my name?"

The Enchanter looked up sharply. "I call you Daughter," he said, "you do not need a name."

She tried another question. "Where is my mother?" she said.

The Enchanter turned pale. "Your mother?" he said. "What do you know of mothers?"

"I have read the books," said his daughter.

Then the Enchanter saw his mistake: for in giving her books he had given her knowledge. For a while he was silent; then he looked at her slyly.

"Daughter," he said, "you have no mother. Once when I was lonely and craved for company, I made you with a powerful spell from a rose that grew on the palace wall."

"Then let me be a rose again," said his daughter, "and I shall know if it is true."

"Very well," said the Enchanter, "but only for a day." He stirred the air with his long, thin fingers and his daughter became a red rose on the south wall of the palace.

She felt the morning dew on her petals as the sun rose through the early mists. She felt the rich perfume drawn out of her by the warm rays as the day went on. She felt the many small feet of a caterpillar which passed over her in the early afternoon, and the gentle movement of the breeze which sprang up at sunset. But deep within her petals there was a strange longing which told her that she was not a rose.

Next morning, she went to the Enchanter and said, "Father, you play games with me. Tell me where my mother is."

The Enchanter saw that she was not deceived.

"You are too clever for me, Daughter," he said, "so I

will tell you the truth. You were once a small bright fish in the shining lake. I caught you on my line in the old days when I had time for such sport. You pleaded for your life, so I made you into a daughter to keep me company."

"Then let me be a fish again," said his daughter, "that I may know my true self."

"For a day then," said the Enchanter, tracing a pattern in the air.

The Enchanter's daughter felt the cool water flowing like silk over her shining scales. She glided through gently swaying forests of green weed.

She leaped up into the bright air and plunged back through a circle of ripples into the mysterious depths. But all the time there were thoughts in her head which told her that she was not a fish.

On the following morning, she went to the Enchanter again and said, "Father, you tease me with your stories. Tell me, please, where my mother is?"

He frowned at her over his books.

"You grow troublesome," he said. "I wish I had not made you into my daughter but had left you a fawn in the forest. For such you were before my spell was cast, and as for your mother, she was a wild deer."

"Then let me be a fawn again," begged his daughter, "that I may run by my mother's side."

At a wave of his hand she felt the dry leaves beneath her tiny hooves and smelled the warm, comforting shelter of the doe beside her. All day, they wandered together through the shade-dappled forest, nibbling young leaves and grazing in sunlit clearings. The doe was gentle and caring and the Enchanter's daughter began to understand what it was to have a mother. And the knowledge stirred old memories deep within her which told her that she was not a fawn.

When she went to her father on the fourth day, she saw that he was growing angry. She knew that she must outwit him if ever she was to find the truth.

"Father," she said, "you have deceived me so far. It is certain that I was never a rose nor a fish nor a fawn in the forest. Why do you hide the truth from me? For surely, if I was none of these, then I must have been a bird before your magic power changed me."

The Enchanter looked at her wearily.

"Why, indeed, so you were," he said, and turned back to his book.

"Let me be a bird again," said his daughter, "for I long once more to be a young eagle on the high summer air."

"You shall be a bird if that is your wish," said the Enchanter. He raised his hand, and as he did so, a faint smile curved his mouth. "But you were never an eagle, my daughter," he said, "only a pretty flying bird." For he read her secret thoughts in her honest eyes and knew that she would escape him if she had the power.

The Enchanter's daughter stretched her tiny wings and rose high above the palace gardens. She flew out across the fields and woods and over the shining lake. She knew she must cross the high white mountains to find her mother, but

for such a journey even an eagle's wings would scarcely have been strong enough. The peaks of the mountains were lost amid the clouds, and as she grew close to them, she was afraid. All day, she flew on over snow-covered wastes and pinnacles of ice and jagged rocks so steep that neither ice nor snow could cling to them.

As the mountains loomed higher, the air grew bitterly cold. Each breath was a struggle and she who had never suffered felt pain for the first time. Darkness fell and she longed to turn back, but the thought of her mother somewhere beyond the mountains put courage into her faint heart and drove her on. By moonlight she crossed the high mountain peaks, only to find more vast snowfields on the other side. Despair seized her as she felt her small strength ebbing away. For she knew that in the morning the spell would be broken and, unable to fly any farther, she would perish in that harsh and inhospitable land.

Then, just as the first light was breaking, she saw a glimpse of green on the far horizon and felt in her frozen body the sudden warmth of hope. With a last effort she flew on toward it, but even as she reached the tree line her tiny wings failed her. Down she fell, down through the branches into the soft snow, and at that very moment the spell was broken.

A young man came up through the forest with a load of firewood and saw, to his astonishment, a girl of great beauty who seemed to lie sleeping in his path. Her clothes were of silk, bright jewels hung about her neck, and her hair flowed like a dark waterfall across the snow. He threw down his load and knelt beside her, but she was stiff and cold. Swiftly he wrapped her in his cloak and carried her away down the mountainside to a small house where smoke rose from a warm fire within.

For many weeks the Enchanter's daughter lay between life and death. She tossed and turned in her fever, and as she did so, she heard a voice in the darkness and dreamed that it was her mother's voice. Sometimes she would feel a cool hand upon her forehead and it seemed to her that it was her mother's hand. The longing of the rose, the thoughts of the little fish, and the memories of the fawn in the forest all seemed to come together, and when at last she opened her eyes she knew that she looked upon her mother's face.

The woman leaning over her had gentle eyes like the doe in the forest. But the Enchanter's daughter saw that they were full of tears.

"Why do you weep?" she asked.

The woman sighed. "Forgive me," she said, "but you bring back the memory of my own daughter who was lost long ago."

"Tell me about her," begged the Enchanter's daughter, for she felt in her heart that it would be her own story.

The woman took her hand. "When I was young," she said, "my husband died, leaving me with a young son and daughter. It was hard for me to work the farm alone, for the mountain land needs a strong hand. One day when I sat weary and sad, a rich man came by on a fine horse, taking the road up into the mountains. He stopped to rest and we made him welcome. My little daughter climbed upon his knee and made him laugh with her childish play. We talked and, learning of our hardship, he offered me gold if I would let him take my daughter for his own. He promised that she should live like a princess, but still I could not part with her.

"The rich man rode on into the mountains while I held my daughter in my arms and watched him go. But the next day she went out to play with her brother on the mountainside and, when night came, she was nowhere to be found. Would that I had let the rich man take her, for then I would know that she still lived somewhere beyond the mountains!"

"What was her name?" asked the Enchanter's daughter, for she knew that she had once had a name and that she would know it again.

"We called her Thi-Phi-Yen," said the woman, "for she was like a pretty flying bird."

When the Enchanter's daughter heard the name, her dreams came back to her. She remembered how the Enchanter had smiled, saying, "You were only a pretty flying bird." And she knew that it was her own name.

Then Thi-Phi-Yen put her arms around her mother's neck and wept for joy. She told her how she had lived as the Enchanter's daughter through the long years and how she had crossed the high white mountains as a small bird to find her.

Thi-Phi-Yen and her mother held each other close to wipe out the memory of the long parting.

"Now I have found you and my brother too," said Thi-Phi-Yen, "and if you will have me, I will never leave you again."

"But we are not rich," said her mother. "We work the farm and live a simple life. You have grown used to jewels and clothes of silk: you have had everything you could desire. You will think our life hard and unrewarding."

"You are wrong, Mother," said Thi-Phi-Yen. "The Enchanter gave me everything except freedom and love: now I have both. No riches can compare with freedom, and no power is greater than love. Am I not your daughter? I can work as hard as you and live as simply. Please tell me that I may stay."

"With all my heart," said her mother, "for life can give me no greater gift."

So it was that the Enchanter's daughter came home again. And from that day she lived happily with her mother and brother at the foot of the high white mountains that lie at the top of the world.

The Story of the Eldest Princess

A. S. BYATT

nce upon a time, in a kingdom between the sea and the mountains, between the forest and the desert, there lived a King and Queen with three daughters. The eldest daughter was pale and quiet, the second daughter was brown and active, and the third was one of those Sabbath daughters who are bonny and bright and good and gay, of whom everything and nothing was expected.

When the eldest Princess was born, the sky was a speedwell blue, covered with very large, lazy, sheep-curly white clouds. When the second Princess was born, there were grey and creamy mares' tails streaming at great speed across the blue. And when the third Princess was born, the sky was a perfectly clear plane of sky-blue, with not a cloud to be seen, so that you might think the blue was spangled with sun-gold, though this was an illusion.

By the time they were young women, things had changed greatly. When they were infants, there were a series of stormy sunsets tinged with sea-green, and seaweed-green. Later there were, as well as the sunsets, dawns, where the sky was mackerel-puckered and underwater-dappled with lime-green and bottle-green and other greens too, malachite and jade. And when they were moody girls the green colours flecked and streaked the blue and the grey all day long, ranging from bronze-greens through emerald to palest opal-greens, with hints of fire. In the early days the people stood in the streets and fields with their mouths open, and said oh, and ah, in tones of admiration and wonder. Then one day a small girl said to her mother that there had been no blue at all for three days now, and she wanted to see blue again. And her mother told her to be sensible and patient and it would blow over, and in about a month the sky was blue, or mostly blue, but only for a few days, and streaked, ominously, the people now felt, with aquamarine. And the blue days were further and further apart, and the greens were more and more varied, until a time when it became quite clear that the fundamental colour of the sky was no longer what they still called sky-blue, but a new sky-green, a pale flat green somewhere between the colours which had once been apple and grass and fern. But of course apple and grass and fern looked very different against this new light, and something very odd and dimming happened to lemons and oranges, and something more savage and hectic to poppies and pomegranates and ripe chillies.

The people, who had at first been entranced, became restive, and, as people will, blamed the King and the Queen for the disappearance of the blue sky. They sent deputations to ask for its return, and they met and muttered in angry knots in the Palace Square. The royal couple consulted each other, and assured each other that they were blameless of greening, but they were uneasy, as it is deep in human nature to suppose human beings, oneself or others, to be responsible for whatever happens. So they consulted the chief ministers, the priests, and a representative sample of generals, witches and wizards. The ministers said nothing could be done, though a contingency-fund might usefully be set up for when a course of action became clear. The priests counselled patience and self-denial, as a general sanative measure, abstention from lentils, and the consumption of more lettuce. The generals supposed it might help to attack their neighbours to the East, since it was useful to have someone else to blame, and the marches and battles would distract the people.

The witches and wizards on the whole favoured a Quest. One rather powerful and generally taciturn wizard, who had interfered very little, but always successfully, in affairs of State, came out of his cavern, and said that someone must be sent along the Road through the Forest across the Desert and into the Mountains, to fetch back the single silver bird and her nest of ash-branches. The bird, he added, was kept in the walled garden of the Old Man of the Mountains, where she sipped from the crystal fountain of life, and was guarded by a thicket of thorns—poisonous thorns—and an interlaced ring of venomous fiery snakes. He believed that advice could be sought along the way about how to elude their vigilance, but the only advice he could give was to keep to the Road, and stray neither in the Forest, nor in the Desert, nor in the rocky paths, and always to be courteous. Then he went back to his cavern.

The King and Queen called together the Council of State, which consisted of themselves, their daughters, the chief minister, and an old duchess, to decide what to do. The Minister advised the Quest, since that was a positive action, which would please the people, and not disrupt the state. The second Princess said she would go of course, and the old duchess went to sleep. The King said he thought it should be done in an orderly manner, and he rather believed that the eldest Princess should go, since she was the first, and could best remember the blue sky. Quite why that mattered so much, no one knew, but it seemed to, and the eldest Princess said she was quite happy to set out that day, if that was what the council believed was the right thing to do.

So she set out. They gave her a sword, and an inexhaustible water-bottle someone had brought back from another Quest, and a package of bread and quails' eggs and lettuce and pomegranates, which did not last very long. They all gathered at the city gate to wish her well, and a trumpeter blew a clear silver sound into the emptiness ahead, and a minister produced a map of the Road, with one or two sketchy patches, especially in the Desert, where its undeviating track tended to be swallowed by sandstorms.

The eldest Princess travelled quickly enough along the Road. Once or twice she thought she saw an old woman ahead of her, but this figure vanished at certain bends and slopes of the path, and did not reappear for some time, and then only briefly, so that it was never clear to the Princess whether there was one, or a succession of old women. In any case, if they were indeed, or she was indeed, an old woman, or old women, she, or they were always very far ahead, and travelling extremely fast.

The Forest stretched along the Road. Pale green glades along its edges, deeper rides, and dark tangled patches beyond these. The Princess could hear but not see birds calling and clattering and croaking in the trees. And occasional butterflies sailed briefly out of the glades towards the Road, busy small scarlet ones, lazily swooping midnight-blue ones, and once, a hand-sized transparent one, a shimmering film of wings with two golden eyes in the centre of the lower wing. This creature hovered over the Road, and seemed to follow the Princess for several minutes, but without ever crossing some invisible barrier between Forest and Road. When it dipped and turned back into the dappled light of the trees the Princess wanted to go after it, to walk on the grass and moss, and knew she must not. She felt a little hungry by now, although she had the inexhaustible water-bottle.

She began to think. She was by nature a reading, not a

travelling princess. This meant both that she enjoyed her new striding solitude in the fresh air, and that she had read a great many stories in her spare time, including several stories about princes and princesses who set out on Quests. What they all had in common, she thought to herself, was a pattern in which the two elder sisters, or brothers, set out very confidently, failed in one way or another, and were turned to stone, or imprisoned in vaults, or cast into magic sleep, until rescued by the third royal person, who did everything well, restored the first and the second, and fulfilled the Quest.

She thought she would not like to waste seven years of her brief life as a statue or prisoner if it could be avoided.

She thought that of course she could be very vigilant, and very courteous to all passers-by—most eldest princesses' failings were failings of courtesy or over-confidence.

There was nobody on the Road to whom she could be courteous, except the old woman, or women, bundling along from time to time a long way ahead.

She thought, I am in a pattern I know, and I suspect I have no power to break it, and I am going to meet a test and fail it, and spend seven years as a stone.

This distressed her so much that she sat down on a convenient large stone at the side of the road and began to weep.

The stone seemed to speak to her in a thin, creaking, dry sort of voice. "Let me out," it said. "I cannot get out." It sounded irritable and angry.

The Princess jumped up. "Who are you?" she cried. "Where are you?"

"I am trapped under this stone," buzzed the voice. "I cannot get out. Roll away the stone."

The Princess put her hands gingerly to the stone and pushed. Pinned underneath it, in a hollow of the ground was a very large and dusty scorpion, waving angry pincers, and somewhat crushed in the tail.

"Did you speak?"

"Indeed I did. I was screaming. It took you an age to hear me. Your predecessor on this Road sat down just here rather heavily when I was cooling myself in this good crack, and pinched my tail, as you see."

"I am glad to have been able to help," said the Princess, keeping a safe distance.

The Scorpion did not answer, as it was trying to raise itself and move forwards. It seemed to move with pain, arching its body and collapsing again, buzzing crossly to itself.

"Can I help?" asked the Princess.

"I do not suppose you are skilled in healing wounds such as mine. You could lift me to the edge of the Forest, where I might be in the path of someone who can heal me, if she ever passes this way again. I suppose *you* are tearing blindly along the Road, like all the rest."

"I am on a Quest, to find the single silver bird in her nest of ash-branches."

"You could put me on a large dock-leaf, and get on your way, then. I expect you are in a hurry."

The Princess looked about for a dock-leaf, wondering whether this irascible creature was her first test, which she was about to fail. She wiped up another tear, and plucked a particularly tough leaf, that was growing conveniently in reach of the Road.

"Good," said the fierce little beast, rearing up and waving its legs. "Quick now, I dislike this hole extremely. Why have you been crying?"

"Because I am not the princess who succeeds, but one of the two who fail and I don't see any way out. You won't force me to be discourteous to you, though I have remarked that your own manners are far from perfect, in that you have yet to thank me for moving the stone, and you order me here and there without saying 'please,' or considering that humans don't like picking up scorpions."

She pushed the leaf towards it as she spoke, and assisted it onto it with a twig, as delicately as she could, though it wriggled and snapped furiously as she did. She put it down in the grass at the edge of the Forest.

"Most scorpions," it observed, "have better things to do than sting at random. If creatures like you stamp on us, then of course we retaliate. Also, if we find ourselves boxed in and afraid. But mostly we have better things to do." It appeared to reflect for a moment. "*If* our tails are not crushed," it added on a dejected note.

"Who is it," the Princess enquired courteously, "who you think can help you?"

"Oh, she is a very wise woman who lives at the other side of the Forest. She would know what to do, but she rarely leaves home and why should she? She has everything she might want where she is. If you were going *that* way, of course, you could carry me a little, until I am recovered. But you are rushing headlong along the Road. Good-bye."

The Princess was rushing nowhere; she was standing very still and thinking. She said:

"I know that story too. I carry you, and ask you, but will you not sting me? And you say, no, it is not in my interest to sting you. And when we are going along, you sting me, although we shall both suffer. And I ask, why did you do that? And you answer—it is my nature."

"You are a very learned young woman, and if we *were* travelling together you could no doubt tell me many instructive stories. I might also point out that I *cannot* sting you— my sting is disabled by the accident to my tail. You may still find me repugnant. Your species usually does. And in any case, you are going along this road, deviating neither to right nor left. Good-bye."

The Princess looked at the Scorpion. Under the dust it was a glistening blue-black, with long arms, fine legs, and complex segments like a jet necklace. Its claws made a crescent before its head. It was not possible to meet its eye, which was disconcerting.

"*I* think you are very handsome."

"Of course I am. I am quick and elegant and versatile and delightfully intricate. I am surprised, however, that you can see it."

The Princess listened only distractedly to this last remark. She was thinking hard. She said, mostly to herself:

"I *could* just walk out of this inconvenient story and go my own way. I *could* just leave the Road and look for my own adventures in the Forest. It would make no difference to the Quest. I should have failed if I left the Road and then the next could set off. Unless of course I got turned into stone for leaving the Road."

"I shouldn't think so," said the Scorpion. "And you could be very helpful to *me*, if you chose, and I know quite a few stories too, and helping other creatures is always a good idea, according to them."

The Princess looked into the Forest. Under the green sky its green branches swayed and rustled in a beckoning way. Its mossy floor was soft and tempting after the dust and grit of the Road. The Princess bent down and lifted up the Scorpion on its leaf and put it carefully into the basket which had contained her food. Then, with a little rebellious skip and jump, she left the Road, and set out into the trees. The Scorpion said she should go south-west, and that if she was hungry it knew where there was a thicket of brambles with early blackberries and a tree-trunk with some mushrooms, so they went in search of those, and the Princess made her mouth black without *quite* assuaging her hunger.

They travelled on, and they travelled on, in a green-arched shade, with the butterflies crowding round the Princess's head and resting on her hair and shoulders. Then they came to a shady clearing, full of grassy stumps and old dry roots, beneath one of which the Princess's keen eye detected a kind of struggling and turbulence in the sand. She stopped to see what it was, and heard a little throaty voice huskily repeating:

"Water. Oh, please, water, if you can hear me, water."

Something encrusted with sand was crawling and flopping over the wiry roots, four helpless legs and a fat little belly. The Princess got down on her knees, ignoring the angry hissing of the Scorpion. Two liquid black eyes peered at her out of the sandy knobs, and a wide mouth opened tremulously and croaked "Water" at her. The Princess brought out her inexhaustible water-bottle and dropped drops into the mouth and washed away the crust of sand, revealing a large and warty green and golden toad, with an unusual fleshy crest on its head. It puffed out its throat and held up its little fingers and toes to the stream of water. As the sand flowed away, it could be seen that there was a large bloody gash on the toad's head.

"Oh, you are hurt," cried the Princess.

"I was caught," said the Toad, "by a Man who had been told that I carry a jewel of great value in my head. So he decided to cut it out. But that is only a story, of course, a human story told by creatures who like sticking coloured stones on their heads and skins, and all I am is flesh and blood. Fortunately for me, my skin is mildly poisonous to Men, so his fingers began to itch and puff up, and I was able to wriggle so hard that he dropped and lost me. But I do not think that I have the strength to make my way back to the person who could heal me."

"We are travelling in her direction," said the Scorpion. "You may travel with us if you care to. You could travel in this Princess's luncheon-basket, which is empty."

"I will come gladly," said the Toad. "But she must not suppose I shall turn into a handsome Prince, or any such nonsense. I am a handsome Toad, or would be, if I had not been hacked at. A handsome Toad is what I shall remain."

The Princess helped it, with a stick, to hop into her

lunch-basket, and continued on through the Forest, in the direction indicated by the Scorpion. They went deeper and darker into the trees, and began to lose sense of there being paths leading anywhere. The Princess was a little tired, but the creatures kept urging her on, to go on as far as possible before night fell. In the growing gloom she almost put her foot on what looked like a ball of thread, blowing out in the roots of some thorny bushes.

The Princess stopped and bent down. *Something* was hopelessly entangled in fine black cotton, dragging itself and the knots that trapped it along in the dust. She knelt on the Forest floor and peered, and saw that it was a giant insect, with its legs and its wing-cases and its belly pulled apart by the snarled threads. The Princess, palace-bred, had never seen such a beast.

"It is a Cockroach," observed the Scorpion. "I thought cockroaches were too clever and tough to get into this sort of mess."

"Those threads are a trap set by the Fowler for singing birds," observed the Toad. "But he has only caught a giant Cockroach."

The Princess disentangled some of the trailing ends, but some of the knots cut into the very substance of the creature, and she feared to damage it further. It settled stoically in the dust and let her move it. It did not speak. The Princess said:

"You had better come with us. We appear to be travelling towards someone who can heal you."

The Cockroach gave a little shudder. The Princess picked it up, and placed it in the basket with the Scorpion and the Toad, who moved away from it fastidiously. It sat, inert, in its cocoon of black thread and said nothing.

They travelled in this way for several days, deeper into the Forest. The creatures told the Princess where to find a variety of nuts, and herbs, and berries, and wild mushrooms she would never have found for herself. Once, a long way off, they heard what seemed to be a merry human whistling, mixed with bird cries. The Princess was disposed to turn in its direction, but the Scorpion said that the whistler was the Fowler, and his calls were designed to entice unwary birds to fly into his invisible nets and to choke there. The Princess, although she was not a bird, was filled with unreasoning fear at this picture, and followed the Scorpion's instructions to creep away, deeper into the thornbushes. On another occasion, again at a distance, she heard the high, throaty sound of a horn, which reminded her of the hunting-parties in the Royal Parks, when the young courtiers would bring down deer and hares and flying fowl with their arrows, and the pretty maidens would clap their hands and exclaim. Again she thought of turning in the direction of the sound, and again, the creatures dissuaded her. For the poor Toad, when he heard the note of the horn, went sludge-grey with fear, and began to quake in the basket.

"That is the Hunter," he said, "who cut at my crest with his hunting-knife, who travels through the wood with cold corpses of birds and beasts strung together and cast over his shoulder, who will aim at a bright eye in a bush for pure fun, and quench it in blood. You must keep away from him." So the Princess plunged deeper still into the thornbushes, though they were tugging at her hair and ripping her dress and scratching her pretty arms and neck.

And one day at noon the Princess heard a loud, clear voice, singing in a clearing, and, peering through a thorn-bush, saw a tall, brown-skinned man, naked to the waist, with black curly hair, leaning on a long axe, and singing:

> *Come live with me and be my love*
> *And share my house and share my bed*
> *And you may sing from dawn to dark*
> *And churn the cream and bake the bread*
> *And lie at night in my strong arms*
> *Beneath a soft goosefeather spread.*

The Princess was about to come out of hiding—he had such a cheery smile, and such handsome shoulders—when a dry

little voice in her basket, a voice like curling wood-shavings rustling, added these lines:

And you may scour and sweep and scrub
With bleeding hands and arms like lead
And I will beat your back, and drive
My knotty fists against your head
And sing again to other girls
To take your place, when you are dead.

"Did you speak?" the Princess asked the Cockroach in a whisper. And it rustled back:

"I have lived in his house, which is a filthy place and full of empty beer-casks and broken bottles. He has five young wives buried in the garden, whom he attacked in his drunken rage. He doesn't kill them, he weeps drunken tears for them, but they lose their will to live. Keep away from the Woodcutter, if you value your life."

The Princess found this hard to believe of the Woodcutter, who seemed so lively and wholesome. She even thought that it was in the creatures' interest to prevent her from lingering with other humans, but nevertheless their warning spoke to something in her that wanted to travel onwards, so she crept quietly away again, and the Woodcutter never knew she had heard his song, or seen him standing there, looking so handsome, leaning on his axe.

They went on, and they went on, deeper into the Forest, and the Princess began to hunger most terribly for bread and butter, touched perhaps by the Woodcutter's Song. The berries she ate tasted more and more watery and were harder and harder to find as the Forest grew denser. The Cockroach seemed inanimate, perhaps exhausted by its effort at speech. The Princess felt bound to hurry, in case its life was in danger, and the other creatures complained from time to time of her clumsiness. Then, one evening, at the moment when the sky was taking on its deepest version of the pine-green that had succeeded dark indigo, the Scorpion begged her to stop and settle down for the night, for its tail ached intolerably. And the Toad added its croaking voice, and begged for more water to be poured over it. The Princess stopped and washed the Toad, and arranged a new leaf for the Scorpion, and said:

"Sometimes I think we shall wander like this, apparently going somewhere, in fact going nowhere, for the rest of our days."

"In which case," rasped the Scorpion, "mine will not be very long, I fear."

"I have tried to help," said the Princess. "But perhaps I should never have left the Road."

And then the flaky voice was heard again.

"If you go on, and turn left, and turn left again, you will see. If you go on now."

So the Princess took up the basket, and put her sandals back on her swollen feet, and went on, and left, and left again. And she saw, through the bushes, a dancing light, very yellow, very warm. And she went on, and saw, at a great distance, at the end of a path knotted with roots and spattered with sharp stones, a window between branches, in which a candle burned steadily. And although she had never in her cossetted life travelled far in the dark, she knew she was seeing, with a huge sense of hope, and warmth and relief, and a minor frisson of fear, what countless benighted travellers had seen before her—though against midnight-blue, not midnight-green—and she felt at one with all those lost homecomers and shelter-seekers.

"It is not the Woodcutter's cottage?" she asked the Cockroach. And it answered, sighing, "No, no, it is the Last House, it is where we are going."

And the Princess went on, running, and stumbling, and hopping, and scurrying, and by and by reached the little house, which was made of mossy stone, with a slate roof over low eaves and a solid wooden door above a white step. There was a good crisp smell of woodsmoke from the chimney. The Princess was suddenly afraid—she had got used to solitude and contriving and going on—but she knocked quickly, and waited.

The door was opened by an old woman, dressed in a serviceable grey dress, with a sharp face covered with intricate fine lines like a spider's web woven of her history, which was both resolute, thoughtful, and smiling. She had sharp green eyes under hooded purple lids, and a plaited crown of wonderful shining hair, iron-grey, silver, and bright white woven together. When she opened the door the Princess almost fainted for the wonderful smell of baking bread that came out, mingled with other delicious smells, baked apples with cinnamon, strawberry tart, just-burned sugar.

"We have been waiting for you," said the Old Woman. "We put the candle in the window for you every night for the last week."

She took the Princess's basket, and led her in. There was a good log fire in the chimney, with a bed of scarlet ash, and there was a long white wooden table, and there were chairs painted in dark bright colours, and everywhere there were eyes, catching the light, blinking and shining. Eyes on the mantelpiece, in the clock, behind the plates on the shelves, jet-black eyes, glass-green eyes, huge yellow eyes, amber eyes, even rose-pink eyes. And what the Princess had taken to be an intricate coloured carpet rustled and moved and shone with eyes, and revealed itself to be a mass of shifting creatures, snakes and grasshoppers, beetles and bumblebees, mice and voles and owlets and bats, a weasel and a few praying mantises. There were larger creatures too—cats and rats and badgers and kittens and a white goat. There was a low, peaceful, lively squeaking and scratching of tiny voices, welcoming and exclaiming. In one corner was a spindle and in another was a loom, and the old lady had just put aside a complicated shawl she was crocheting from a rainbow-coloured basket of scraps of wool.

"One of you needs food," said the Old Woman, "and three of you need healing."

So the Princess sat down to good soup, and fresh bread, and fruit tart with clotted cream and a mug of sharp cider, and the Old Woman put the creatures on the table, and healed them in her way. Her way was to make them tell the story of their hurts, and as they told, she applied ointments and drops with tiny feathery brushes and little bone pins, uncurling and splinting the Scorpion's tail as it rasped out the tale of its injuries, swabbing and stitching the Toad's wounded head with what looked like cobweb threads, and unknotting the threads that entwined the Cockroach with almost invisible hooks and tweezers. Then she asked the Princess for her story, which the Princess told as best she could, living again the moment when she realized she was doomed to fail, imitating the Scorpion's rasp, and the Toad's croaking gulp, and the husky whisper of the Cockroach. She brought the dangers of the Forest into the warm fireside, and all the creatures shuddered at the thought of the Hunter's arrow, the Fowler's snare, and the Woodman's axe. And the Princess, telling the story, felt pure pleasure in getting it right, making it just so, finding the right word, and even— she went so far—the right gesture to throw shadow-branches and shadow-figures across the flickering firelight and the yellow pool of candlelight on the wall. And when she had finished there was all kinds of applause, harmonious wing-scraping, and claw-tapping, and rustling and chirruping.

"You are a born storyteller," said the old lady. "You had the sense to see you were caught in a story, and the sense to see that you could change it to another one. And the special wisdom to recognize that you are under a curse—which is also a blessing—which makes the story more interesting to you than the things that make it up. There are young women who would never have listened to the creatures' tales about the Woodman, but insisted on finding out for themselves. And maybe they would have been wise and maybe they would have been foolish: that is *their* story. But you listened to the Cockroach and stepped aside and came here, where we collect stories and spin stories and mend what we can and investigate what we can't, and live quietly without striving to change the world. We have no story of our own here, we are free, as old women are free, who don't have to worry about princes or kingdoms, but dance alone and take an interest in the creatures."

"But——" said the Princess, and stopped.

"But?"

"But the sky is still green and I have failed, and I told the story to suit myself."

"The green is a very beautiful colour, or a very beautiful range of colours, I think," said the old lady. "Here, it gives us pleasure. We write songs about greenness and make tapestries with skies of every possible green. It adds to the beauty of the newt and the lizard. The Cockroach finds it restful. Why should things be as they always were?"

The Princess did not know, but felt unhappy. And the creatures crowded round to console her, and persuade her to live quietly in the little house, which was what she wanted to do, for she felt she had come home to where she was free. But she was worried about the sky and the other princesses. Then the Cockroach chirped to the old lady:

"Tell us the rest of the story, tell us the end of the story, of the story the Princess left."

He was feeling decidedly better already, his segments were eased, and he could bend almost voluptuously.

"Well," said the old lady, "this is the story of the eldest Princess. But, as you percipiently observe, you can't have the story of the eldest, without the stories of the next two, so I will tell you those stories, or possible stories, for many things may and do happen, stories change themselves, and these stories are not histories and have not happened. So you may believe my brief stories about the middle one and the youngest or not, as you choose."

"I always believe stories whilst they are being told," said the Cockroach.

"You are a wise creature," said the Old Woman. "That is what stories are for. And after, we shall see what we shall see." So she told

THE BRIEF STORY OF THE SECOND PRINCESS

When the second Princess realized that the first was not returning, she too set out, and met identical problems and pleasures, and sat down on the same stone, and realized that she was caught in the same story. But being a determined young woman, she decided to outwit the story, and went on, and after many adventures was able to snatch the single silver bird in her nest of branches and return in triumph to her father's palace. And the old wizard told her that she must light the branches and burn the bird, and although she felt very uneasy about this she was determined to do as she should, so she lit the fire. And the nest and the bird were consumed, and a new glorious bird flew up from the conflagration, and swept the sky with its flaming tail, and everything was blue, as it had once been. And the Princess became Queen when her parents died, and ruled the people wisely, although they grumbled incessantly because they missed the variety of soft and sharp greens they had once been able to see.

THE BRIEF STORY OF THE THIRD PRINCESS

As for the third Princess, when the bird flamed across the sky, she went into the orchard and thought, I have no need to go on a Quest. I have nothing I must do, I can do what I like. I have no story. And she felt giddy with the empty space around her, a not entirely pleasant feeling. And a frisky little wind got up and ruffled her hair and her petticoats and blew bits of blossom all over the blue sky. And the Princess had the idea that she was tossed and blown like the petals of the cherry-trees. Then she saw an old woman, with a basket, at the gate of the orchard. So she walked towards her and when she got there, the Old Woman told her, straight out,

"You are unhappy because you have nothing to do."

So the Princess saw that this was a wise old woman, and answered politely that this was indeed the case.

"I might help," said the Old Woman. "Or I might not. You may look in my basket."

In the basket were a magic glass which would show the Princess her true love, wherever he was, whatever he was doing, and a magic loom that made tapestries that would live on the walls of the palace chambers as though they were thickets of singing birds, and Forest rides leading to the edge of vision.

"Or I could give you a thread," said the Old Woman as the Princess hesitated, for she did not want to see her true love, not yet, not just yet, he was the *end* of stories not begun, and she did not want to make magic Forests, she wanted to see real ones. So she watched the old lady pick up from the grass the end of what appeared to be one of those long, trailing gossamer threads left by baby spiders travelling on the air in the early dawn. But it was as strong as linen thread, and as fine as silk, and when the Old Woman gave it a little tug it tugged tight and could be seen to run away, out of the orchard, over the meadow, into the woods and out of sight.

"You gather it in," said the Old Woman, "and see where it takes you."

The thread glittered and twisted, and the Princess began to roll it neatly in, and took a few steps along it, and gathered it, and rolled it into a ball, and followed it, out of the orchard, across the meadow, and into the woods, and . . . but that is another story.

"Tell me one thing," said the eldest Princess to the Old Woman when they had all applauded her story. The moon shone in an emerald sky, and all the creatures drowsed and rustled. "Tell me one thing. Was that you, ahead of me in the road, in such a hurry?"

"There is always an old woman ahead of you on a journey, and there is always an old woman behind you too, and they are not always the same, they may be fearful or kindly, dangerous or delightful, as the road shifts, and you speed along it. Certainly I was ahead of you, and behind you too, but not only I, and not only as I am now."

"I am happy to be here with you as you are now."

"Then that is a good place to go to sleep, and stop telling stories until the morning, which will bring its own changes."

So they went to bed, and slept until the sun streaked the apple-green horizon with grassy-golden light.

The Outspoken Princess

DOV MIR

t was said that King Hickory and Queen Gadonia had been made from a devil's brew and a witch's mean mood. Whatever the truth may be, they were so ferocious and spiteful that even the fairies were afraid of them and stayed as far as possible from their kingdom.

Now, a kingdom without the grace and protection of fairies is a kingdom without hope. So, King Hickory and Queen Gadonia were free to rule as ruthlessly as they wished, and it appeared that there was no end to their lust for power.

Since they loved diamonds almost as much as they loved their own power, they formed a militia of merciless Nabobs to force the people of their kingdom to work in the royal mines and factories. Though their people suffered, the king and queen showed no concern just as long as they themselves could enjoy their glittery diamond castle built on top of a glass mountain.

Once, when their people rebelled because there was nothing to eat, Hickory declared, "Let them eat weeds!"

And Gadonia laughed, "They're nothing but vegetables anyway."

And they sent the bellicose Nabobs to whip the people back to the mines and factories.

As their nasty fame increased and their army of truculent Nabobs grew stronger, Hickory and Gadonia conquered other lands, and foreign rulers had to travel from all over the world to pay their respects and admire their castle. Yet, despite all their power and diamonds, King Hickory and Queen Gadonia became more sinister with each year that passed, and it was said that their cruelty would increase unless they had a son to inherit their throne.

For many years they had tried in vain to give birth to a son, and since they were convinced that nothing could be wrong with them, they blamed the fairies for their bad luck. Finally, they lost their patience and sent their Nabobs out into the world to kidnap some fairies, for they knew that fairy magic was their only hope to have a son.

Equipped with the latest radar devices, the Nabobs managed to capture three fairies within a week and threw them into a prison cell built with electronic wires to keep the fairies from disappearing into thin air or flying away. Not even their magic wands could help them.

"Give us a baby, or you stay here for the rest of your lives!" Queen Gadonia warned them.

"And it better be soon, or we'll clip your wings once a week," King Hickory added with a sadistic smile.

"Yes, good idea," the queen hissed.

The fairies were terrified, and after putting their heads together, they delivered their response.

"A child you shall have," they said. "It will be a wonderful child, a miracle child, who will change your lives. But you must promise never to harm this child no matter what happens. If you do, you shall lose your kingdom and all your evil powers."

Queen Gadonia and King Hickory agreed, but they added, "No tricks, or we'll get even with you!"

"No tricks," the fairies promised.

"And no waiting nine months," Gadonia said. "I can't stand long pregnancies or labor pains."

"Seven days," the fairies said. "Seven days and your miracle child will arrive."

So the fairies were released, and seven days passed. The queen went to the royal hospital because she felt a slight rumbling in her stomach. Sure enough, she was pregnant and about to give birth, but neither the king nor the queen had expected what was to come.

Certainly, they had expected a cry, a sigh, or howl, but not,

"Please, open the windows! It's boiling in here!"

And not complete sentences. Above all, they had not

expected a daughter. But that was what the little baby was—a daughter who was totally frank and totally outspoken.

After a nurse wrapped her in a blanket and held her up for all to see, she looked at her mother and father and smiled with big dimples. However, their only response was a nasty glare.

"The least you could do is smile." The little girl tried to warm up to them. "I'm your daughter. Millicent's my name."

But the king and queen refused to talk to her. They were furious. They had wanted a son, a silent, handsome son, not a talking princess. So, they simply stared and let her talk about her birth and amaze the doctor and nurses who were so delighted that they wanted to keep Millicent in the hospital for further observation. A genius had been born. Millicent was a scientific sensation. The newspapers printed all the details of her miraculous birth. The radio announcers could not stop reporting about the historical event, and the television and camera crews wanted to interview the royal couple and especially their baby. But Millicent said, "No!"

It was not a nasty "no," but a firm one. "No" to the doctors, "no" to the radio reporters, "no" to the television crews. Millicent wanted her privacy and wanted to get to know her parents.

But Millicent knew her own mind too much for the king and queen to bear. At least, this is what the king and queen began to feel when they brought her to the nursery and placed her in a crib decorated in pink velvet. The entire room had been quickly prepared for her: pink wallpaper with blond angels; cuddly stuffed brown bears and white fluffy rabbits; smiling baby dolls stuck on shelves with lovely rosy cheeks and golden locks of hair.

"If you don't mind," Millicent said as politely as she could, "I really don't like pink. I'd like to do my own decorating."

Queen Gadonia broke into tears. Despite her hard heart, she could not bear a daughter who spoke her own mind, and she ran sobbing from the room. King Hickory grumbled but controlled his temper and ordered three well-groomed governesses to take turns looking after Millicent while he ran to comfort his wife.

THE NEXT DAY, when the king and queen approached the nursery, they could hear hammering and sawing. There was such a racket that they thought the castle might be collapsing. Instead, they found Millicent, but it was not the same daughter they had met the day before. Millicent had grown four years overnight. She now had long curly brown hair and sparkling green eyes, and she leaned over the edge of her crib and gave orders to seven lean but strong carpenters in torn jeans and overalls, while the governesses, locked in a wooden cage, looked on with helpless smiles.

"What is going on here?" the king roared.

One of the carpenters pointed to Millicent and kept on working. King Hickory looked over to his daughter who was smiling and hoping that her parents would like her new decorations.

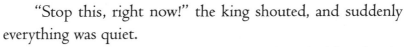

"Stop this, right now!" the king shouted, and suddenly everything was quiet.

"What do you think you're doing?" he asked his daughter.

Millicent was hurt but tried to be as pleasant as she could. "I didn't think you'd mind," she said. "The room needed a face-lift, and these poor people needed some work."

"We didn't give you permission," the king answered.

"I really didn't mean to upset you," Millicent said.

"Of course you've upset us. You're changing everything!" the queen said, and pointed to what was left of the nursery.

"But I thought you'd like it," Millicent responded frankly.

"Don't you talk back to me, young lady!" the queen exclaimed and turned to her husband. "She takes after your side of the family."

"My side!" the king responded. "She's got your wicked tongue and your stubbornness."

"Your side!" the queen insisted.

"Yours!" the king persisted.

"Please, I don't want to belong to either side," Millicent intervened. "I don't want to take sides."

But that remark was once again too frank for Queen Gadonia to bear, and tears flooded her cheeks. She turned and ran from the room, prompting King Hickory to yell at Millicent, "I should give you a good spanking!" But he remembered what the fairies had said and controlled his temper.

*　　*　　*

THE NEXT DAY the king and queen agreed not to quarrel but to make the best of what they thought was now a bad situation. So, they marched to Millicent's nursery, pleased that they did not hear the banging and bamming they had heard the other day. But when they opened the door to their daughter's room, they could not believe their eyes.

Millicent and seven boys and girls were painting pictures of fairies on all the walls. Fairies with magic wands. Fairies fighting dragons. Fairies flying through the sky. Fairies bringing gifts and food to the people of the kingdom.

"Stop this!" King Hickory yelled.

"Your room is a mess," Queen Gadonia added, "and you've grown another year."

"We forbid you to grow!" the king said.

"And we forbid you to paint, especially in the palace," the queen added again.

"But we were just having fun," Millicent responded.

"Princesses aren't born to have fun," the queen reminded her.

"You were born to rule!" the king stated. "Now, get rid of your friends. It's time we had a talk, young lady. It's time to teach you some manners."

The king and queen turned and left the room, and Millicent shook her head slowly. It was difficult to please her parents and sort out her feelings. But right then and there she had little time to do anything. The well-groomed governesses showed up shortly after the king and queen

had left her room and began instructing her when to say "yes" and when to say "no," what to wear, how to move, what fork, knife, and spoon to use, when to get up and when to go to bed, what TV programs to watch, and what children were to be her friends. The governesses took turns drilling her, and by the end of the day, Millicent was exhausted.

"Not another day like this," she said to herself as her head hit the pillow. "I've got to save myself."

THAT NIGHT MILLICENT tossed and turned, and when she woke up, she had grown another five years.

"What am I going to do?" she asked herself, but it was too late. The three governesses had already arrived to give her sewing and cooking lessons. When they saw how much she had grown, they immediately took her to the royal throne room.

"What do you think you're doing, young lady?" Queen Gadonia asked.

"I'm sorry, Mother," Millicent said. "But I don't—"

"Your Highness," the queen interrupted. "You're to call me Your Highness, not Mother."

"I'm sorry, Your Highness," Millicent continued, "but I really didn't mean to grow."

"Do you think we're stupid?" the queen asked. "You're obviously using fairy magic."

"Fairy magic?!" Millicent exclaimed. "I've never seen a fairy in my life."

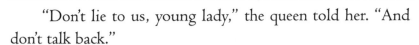

"Don't lie to us, young lady," the queen told her. "And don't talk back."

"But I'm telling you the truth," Millicent said.

"Well, perhaps you are," the king responded. "But if you grow any more or say one word to us without our permission, you'll be banished from the kingdom. No more growing, and no more talking back to us."

"I'll try," Millicent said.

"You'd better do more than try," the queen insisted. "You already grow too much and speak too much."

Millicent wanted to say something, but she was afraid because the king and queen bared their teeth that were capped with diamonds, and their glittering mouths seemed sharper and more dangerous than the bite of a shark.

"Take her away!" the king barked.

The governesses took Millicent to a sewing room, and there she was forced to sew and knit diamond scarves for her mother in total silence. In the meantime, King Hickory and Queen Gadonia began having a serious discussion about the fate of their only daughter.

"I don't trust her," King Hickory said. "There's too much of the fairy spirit in her."

"You're right," the queen agreed. "What would happen if we died, and she became queen. She'd probably sell our diamond castle and give away everything we've worked so hard for."

"She has to disappear," the king said.

"But if we harm her, we'll lose our kingdom and all our power," the queen reminded her husband.

"We don't have to harm her," the king replied. "She just has to disappear like some other people who have bothered us."

THE NEXT DAY, Millicent woke up and could not believe that she had grown another year.

"You've broken your promise!" the king exclaimed.

"Twelve years old!" the queen joined in. "How dare you!"

"But," Millicent tried to explain.

"And you're speaking back!" The queen pointed her finger at her. "It's clear you're not fit to be our daughter, and since you can't prove otherwise, you're now banished from our sight forever!"

"Take her away!" the king commanded.

Then Hickory and Gadonia called for three coldhearted Nabobs and commanded them to take Millicent deep into the dark city slums and abandon her, knowing full well that a girl of twelve would never be able to survive in the jungle of the city.

Millicent was nervous and anxious. Although she was indeed twelve, she had only been on earth for a few days and was not familiar with the city. As the Nabobs led her through the streets, she could not help but notice the poor and starving people asking for handouts, the trash on the streets, the broken windows and doors of buildings. What a difference from the splendid diamond castle! And the people in the streets looked at her in such a threatening way. She tried smiling at them, but they did not respond.

"Wait here!" one of the Nabobs said when they came to a small brick building. "We must get something inside."

The Nabobs went into the building while Millicent remained outside. However, they did not return. Instead, they ran out a backdoor and returned to the castle, leaving Millicent to her fate. The poor girl began to shiver. It was a cold spring evening, and there was a chill in the air. Millicent waited one hour, two hours, and after the third hour she went inside and realized that she had been tricked. A tear slid down her cheek. "I didn't deserve this," Millicent thought to herself.

"No, you didn't," a voice responded behind her.

Millicent quickly turned around, and standing before her were three old women dressed in rags.

"And we haven't deserved to be treated as beggars either," one of the women said.

"Who are you?" Millicent asked.

"Don't be afraid, child," the third woman said. "We've come to help you."

"Yes, we've come to help," another one said. "We've stayed away from this kingdom too long, and it's time to return."

They took her hand and led her out of the building. As she stood between them, the moon cast its warm rays on her face, and she smiled. And when she walked with the three women through the streets, the people came out of their buildings and returned her smile. It was as if she had always belonged there.

Millicent continued walking through the city, and when she reached the center, she stopped. A large crowd of people gathered around her. One of the beggar women handed her a large paintbrush, and another, some sparkling silver paint. Millicent began painting a huge diamond in the middle of the city, and the people stood on its borders, watching her. When she was done, she walked to the center of the diamond accompanied by the three beggar women. "Come and help me trample this diamond!" Millicent spoke out.

The people were silent. They didn't know what to do. Some thought she might be a little crazy. No one moved.

Then Millicent marched to the edge of the diamond and began trampling its borders. Soon her trampling turned into a dance, and there was music in the air. She signaled the people to join her. But they were scared and stepped back from her until a child sprung forward and took hold of her hand and began dancing on the diamond. She was followed by her mother and some other children, who began to laugh and trample the diamond. And it was their laughter that set the other people free. Soon they all began dancing on the diamond and did not notice when Millicent left them alone and went off with the three old beggars.

However, Millicent did not disappear from the city. Much to the irritation of her parents, she began working in the royal factories and mines. She worked in hospitals and shelters. She wrote articles for newspapers and magazines. She played a guitar and sang folksongs for little children. She joined the firefighters and helped the farmers during the harvest season. Millicent could be seen everywhere, and nobody knew how she did what she did, except perhaps the three strange women with whom she lived.

"WE MUST PUT AN end to this!" The king and queen were upset, and they issued a proclamation forbidding anyone to hire princesses to work for them, especially banished princesses.

But they could not stop Millicent from growing. And grow she did. Not as quickly as she had done before. It actually took her three years to grow three years, but those three years were three years of trouble for King Hickory and Queen Gadonia.

Everyone in the kingdom kept asking why they had banished such a wonderful daughter. And everyone kept wondering whether there was something wrong with the king and queen. Of course, nobody dared to say this in public because they were afraid of the Nabobs. That is, until the day Millicent began giving out diamonds.

"Diamonds for free!" she cried out.

"You can't do this," a Nabob said.

"Who said?" Millicent asked.

"Why, uh . . ." the Nabob stuttered.

"Here, take one!" Millicent offered the Nabob a diamond.

The Nabob smiled and took the diamond, and Millicent continued on her way.

"Diamonds for free!"

Not only did she give diamonds to the people but also to the Nabobs, who became so confused by their sudden wealth that they stopped threatening people in the city. What's more, Millicent began wearing clothes that had a trampled diamond sewn on them as a badge.

"Trampled diamonds for free!" she cried out, and she

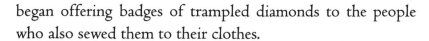

began offering badges of trampled diamonds to the people who also sewed them to their clothes.

WHEN THE KING and queen heard about this, they were furious and summoned Millicent to the palace. At first she refused to come, but then the king and queen sent out two of their more vicious Nabobs, who dragged her to the castle.

"Well!" King Hickory said when Millicent appeared before the throne. "What do you think you're doing?"

"Nobody wants to work for us anymore, now that they have their own diamonds," Queen Gadonia added. "How do you expect us to rule?"

Millicent remained silent.

"Has the cat got your tongue?" Queen Gadonia asked.

"Speak!" the king commanded.

"Tell us what's on your mind," the queen added. "After all, you've always been outspoken."

But Millicent kept quiet and just stared at Hickory and Gadonia.

"I'm losing my temper," the king said.

"Me, too," the queen remarked.

Still no words from Millicent.

"That does it!" the king exploded, and he jumped down from the throne and slapped Millicent's face. "I'm going to slap you silly until you talk!"

But as he raised his right arm to hit Millicent again, he felt paralyzed. He could not move, nor could the queen. They could only watch as three old women suddenly

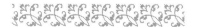 

appeared. They seemed to be beggars. Yet, the rags they were wearing were made of silk, and their strong gaze held the king and the queen in check.

"You've broken your promise," one of them said.

"You've lost your powers," said another.

"We're back to stay," the third woman said.

Of course, the king and queen could not reply because they had been transformed into statues, and their monstrous Nabobs soon became gigantic trees providing shade for people throughout the kingdom.

Greater changes took place when Millicent became queen. She ordered the castle of diamonds to be torn down and the diamonds to be shared among the people of the kingdom. The statues of King Hickory and Queen Gadonia were carried to a large green garden that Millicent turned into a park where everyone was allowed to give speeches and say whatever they wanted. The people called it "Speakers' Park," and it was in this park that Millicent spoke out in front of the statues of the king and queen and granted free elections to the people. Rumor has it that Millicent was elected the first president of what had once been a kingdom of fear and terror. But that was long ago, and we do not know everything for sure. We only know that hope returned to that kingdom as soon as Millicent began speaking out.

PERMISSIONS

BIOGRAPHIES

Alexander, Lloyd (1924–   ) Born in Philadelphia, Alexander studied at Lafayette College and the Sorbonne and first made a name for himself as the translator of Jean-Paul Sartre and other French authors. During the 1960s he turned to writing children's fiction and became recognized as one of the most gifted American writers of fantasy with his Prydain cycle, which includes *The Book of Three* (1964), *The Black Cauldron* (1965), *The Castle of Llyr* (1966), *Taran Wanderer* (1967), and *The High King* (1968). As a complement to this cycle, he published *The Foundling and Other Tales* in 1973. One of the most prolific and inventive authors of fantasy in America, Alexander has published over forty books and won such awards as the Newbery Medal (1968), the National Book Award (1970), and the American Book Award (1981). Among his best works are: *The Marvelous Misadventures of Sebastian* (1970), *The Cat Who Wished to Be a Man* (1973), *The First Two Lives of Lukas-Kasha* (1978), *Westmark* (1981), *The*

Illyrian Adventure (1986), and *The Philadelphia Adventure* (1990). "The Cat-King's Daughter" was first published in *The Town Cats and Other Tales* (1977).

Barber, Antonia is a pseudonym of Barbara Anthony (1932–   ). Born in London, Anthony studied at University College in London and began publishing books for children in 1966. Her second book, *The Ghosts* (1969), was nominated for a Carnegie Award. After taking time out to raise three children, Anthony returned to writing with the publication of *The Ring in the Old Stuff* (1983). In addition, she has also done a series of "Satchelmouse" books. "The Enchanter's Daughter" was first published in 1987.

Byatt, Antonia S. (1936–   ) Born in Sheffield and educated at Cambridge, she is the author of such outstanding novels as *The Shadow of the Sun* (1964), *The Game* (1967), *The Virgin in the Garden* (1978), *Still Life* (1980), and *Possession* (1990), winner of the Booker Prize. She has also published a collection of stories, *Sugar and Other Stories,* and has had a distinguished career as a lecturer, critic, and broadcaster. Byatt has also taught as a lecturer and senior lecturer at London University from 1975 to 1983 and has published such significant scholarly works as *Degrees of Freedom: The Novels of Iris Murdoch* (1965) and *Wordsworth and Coleridge in Their Time* (1970). "The Story of the Eldest Princess" was first published in the anthology *Caught in a Story* (1992), edited by Christine Park and Caroline Heaton.

Coombs, Patricia (1926–   ) Born in Los Angeles, she received her B.A. and M.A. from the University of Washington and established a name for herself with her "Dorrie" series about a spunky young girl witch whose hat is always crooked and socks never match. Begun in 1962 with *Dorrie's Magic*, Coombs has written and illustrated sixteen sequels up to *Dorrie and the Witchville Fair* (1980). In addition, she has also written and illustrated several other unusual and imaginative books for children such as *The Lost Playground* (1963), *Lisa and the Grompet* (1970), *Mouse Cafe* (1972), *The Magic Pot* (1977), *Tillabel* (1978), and *The Magic McTree* (1983). "Molly Mullett" was first published in 1975.

Corbalis, Judy (1941–   ) Born in Dannevirke, New Zealand, where she studied at Victoria University, she first came to Great Britain on an eighteen-month working holiday and remained. After attending the London Academy of Music and Dramatic Art, she worked in television, fringe and community theater, an opera company, and music hall. *The Wrestling Princess and Other Stories* was her first book and was selected in the Feminist Book Fortnight 1986 as one of their top twenty books of the year. She has since published more unique fantasy books for young readers such as *Porcellus, Flying Pig* (1987), *Oskar and the Icepick* (1988), and *The Cuckoo Bird* (1988) and has worked on the television adaptation of some of her tales. "The Wrestling Princess" is the title story of her book by the same name.

Gardner, John (1933–1982) Born in Batavia, New York, Gardner studied at Washington University and Iowa State University, where he received his Ph.D. in 1958. He taught medieval literature and creative writing at a number of colleges and universities and eventually became the founder and director of the writing program at the State University of New York at Binghamton from 1978 to 1982, when he died in a motorcycle accident. His compelling and brilliant fiction—including *Grendel* (1971), *Nickel Mountain* (1973), *The King's Indian and Other Fireside Tales*, *The Art of Living and Other Stories* (1981), and *Mikkelson's Ghost* (1982)—has earned him a respected place in contemporary American literature. In 1975, with the publication of *Dragon, Dragon and Other Timeless Tales*, he turned his attention to fairy tales and books for young readers. He followed that book with other splendid fairy-tale works such as *Gudgekin the Thistle Girl and Other Tales* (1976), *In the Suicide Mountains* (1977), and *King of the Hummingbirds and Other Tales* (1977).

Hemingway, Ernest (1899–1961) Born in Oak Park, Illinois, he joined the army during World War I and served as an ambulance driver in France and Italy. When he returned to the States in 1919, he began working as a newspaper reporter and soon returned to France as a correspondent. His first works of fiction, *Three Stories and Ten Poems* (1923), *In Our Time* (1924), and *The Torrents of Spring* (1926), drew very little attention, but with the publication of *The Sun Also Rises* (1926) he became recognized as the foremost writer of the "lost generation" of American writers. Today he is considered anything but "lost." Rather, with such works as *A Farewell to Arms* (1929), *To Have and Have Not* (1937), *For Whom the Bell Tolls* (1940), and *The Old Man and the Sea* (1952) and stories like "The Killers" and "The Snows of Kilimanjaro," he has taken his place among the contemporary classical writers. "The Faithful Bull," a rare fairy tale by Hemingway, was first published in 1951.

Kennedy, Richard (1932–   ) Born in Jefferson City, Missouri, he studied at Portland State and Oregon State universities, and aside from a brief period from 1951 to 1954 when he served in the U.S. Air Force, Kennedy has spent most of his life in Oregon. He has held a variety of jobs ranging from elementary-school teacher to woodcutter and fireman, and since 1974 he has been the custodian at the Oregon State University Marine Center. During the early 1970s Kennedy began writing fairy tales and books for children, and among his best works are two novels for adolescents, *The Boxcar at the Center of the Universe* (1982) and *Amy's Eyes* (1985). His finely crafted fairy tales have appeared in journals and as separate books and were brought together in his *Collected Stories* (1987), which included "The Dark Princess," first published in 1978.

Lee, Tanith (1947–   ) Born in London, she was educated at Croydon Art School and began writing fairy tales and science fiction during the 1970s. She is considered one of the leading writers of fantasy in Great Britain today. She has written two outstanding works for young readers, *The Dragon Hoard* (1971) and *Princess Hynchatti and Some Other Surprises* (1972), and among her best fantasy and science fiction works for adults are: *The Birthgrave* (1975), *The Quest for the White Witch* (1979), *Electric Forest* (1979), *The Gorgon and Other Beastly Tales* (1985), *Women as Demons* (1989), and *Blood of Roses* (1990). Her book *Red as Blood or Tales from the Grimmer Sisters* (1983) deserves special mention as an innovative collection of traditional fairy tales written from a feminist perspective that subverts the classical tradition. "Princess Dahli" was originally published in *Princess Hynchatti* and is more optimistic than the tales in *Red as Blood*.

Mir, Dov (1960–   ) Born in Kiev, Ukraine, he moved to Moscow as a young boy and, fluent in five languages, he later studied comparative literature at the University of Moscow. During his student years he began publishing short stories for children that appeared in various Russian journals. "Micha and the Bumbling Giant" (1983), "The Crumbling Wall" (1984), and "The Sorrowful Smile of Princess Liliane" (1984) are among his best. His intriguing fantasy novella *Jacob the Spy* (1985) appeared shortly before Mir became foreign correspondent for a Kiev newspaper in France. Due to political difficulties, he remained in Paris and then moved to New York in 1987. Since settling in the States, he has continued to work as a journalist and has also begun to write children's books and works of fantasy. "The

Outspoken Princess" was adapted in 1992 from a tale that Mir originally wrote in Russian.

Schickel, Richard (1933–   ) Born in Milwaukee, Wisconsin, Schickel attended the University of Wisconsin, and he has since then been active in journalism, cinema, and television. Early in his career he was a reporter on *Sports Illustrated,* a senior editor on *Look* and *Show,* and, as a freelance writer, has contributed to over a dozen national magazines. He is perhaps best known now as a film critic for *Time* magazine and as the author of over twenty books mainly about the movies. Among his best books are *The Disney Version* (1968), one of the first serious studies of Disney's life and works; *D. W. Griffith: An American Life* (1984), the definitive biography of the pioneering film director; *Schickel on Film* (1989); *Brando: A Life in Our Times* (1991); and *"Double Indemnity"* (1992). In addition to his work as a critic and television producer, he has also lectured at Yale and the University of Southern California. Schickel wrote his one and only remarkable fairy tale, "The Gentle Knight," in 1964.

Sendak, Jack (1923–   ) Born in Brooklyn, he served in the U.S. Army during World War II and began writing children's books in the 1950s. His first two books, *The Happy Rain* (1956) and *Circus Girl* (1958), were illustrated by his brother Maurice. Among his other works are *The Second Witch* (1965), *Martze* (1968), and *The Magic Tears* (1971), which was selected as the *New York Times* Choice of Best Illustrated

Children's Books of the Year. "The Signal" was published in his wonderful collection *The King of the Hermits and Other Stories* (1966), which contains several tales with a bizarre and charming Central European atmosphere.

Storr, Catherine (1913–   ) Born in London, Storr studied at Cambridge and later at West London Hospital. She qualified as a physician in 1947 and specialized in psychiatry. In 1948 Storr began working as a psychiatrist in West London Hospital and was appointed the Senior Hospital Medical Officer in the Department of Psychological Medicine in 1950 in Middlesex Hospital, where she remained until 1962. She also worked as an editor for Penguin Books and is presently retired. In 1951 she created the Clever Polly Series for children to project a positive image of independent girls in fantasy literature and published *Clever Polly and the Stupid Wolf* in 1955 and *Polly, the Giant's Bride* in 1956. She has published over thirty-five books for children and adults. Among her best fairy-tale books are: *The Chinese Egg* (1975), *The Painter and the Fish* (1975), *The Boy and the Swan* (1987), *Daljit and the Unqualified Wizard* (1990), and *Last Stories of Polly and the Wolf* (1990).

Williams, Jay (1914–1978) Born in Buffalo, New York, Williams was educated at the University of Pennsylvania and Columbia University. He worked in vaudeville shows and as a nightclub comic in the Catskill Mountains and then as a Hollywood press agent before joining the U.S. Army in

1941. After his discharge in 1945, he began writing stories full-time and published seventy-six books of fiction and non-fiction for adults and children. He is perhaps best known for his popular science fiction series, the Danny Dunn books. Under the pen name Michael Delving he wrote a number of crime novels. Among his best books for children are *The Sword and the Scythe* (1946), *The Magic Gate* (1949), *The Cookie Tree* (1967), *The King with Six Friends* (1968), *The Good-for-Nothing Prince* (1969), *School for Sillies* (1969), *Everyone Knows What a Dragon Looks Like* (1976), and *The Reward Worth Having* (1977). "Petronella" was published in *The Practical Princess and Other Liberating Fairy Tales* (1978).

Yolen, Jane (1939–   ) Born in New York City, Yolen was educated at Smith College. After working in publishing she became a freelance writer in 1965 and soon established a reputation as a writer of remarkable fairy tales for children such as *Gwinellen, the Princess Who Could Not Sleep* (1965), *The Emperor and the Kite* (1968), *The Girl Who Loved the Wind* (1972), *The Girl Who Cried Flowers* (1974), and *The Moon Ribbon and Other Tales* (1976). It was also during this time that she began teaching at Smith College and writing nonfiction about fantasy and children's literature. In 1983 many of Yolen's unusual fairy tales for children and adults were collected and published in *Tales of Wonder*, and she began experimenting more in the field of fantasy. Some of her best fantasy narratives for adults can be found in *Dragonfield* (1985) and *Merlin's Booke* (1986). She has also written highly original fairy-tale novels such as *Briar Rose* (1993), which, like *The Devil's Arithmetic* (1988), deals compellingly with the Holocaust. In addition, Yolen has also written a critical study of fairy tales entitled *Touch Magic* (1983) and has edited *Favorite Folktales from Around the World* (1986). "The White Seal Maid" was first published in 1977 in *The Hundredth Dove and Other Tales.*

ABOUT THE EDITOR

JACK ZIPES is professor of German at the University of Minnesota, in Minneapolis, and has previously held professorships at New York University, the University of Munich, the University of Berlin, the University of Frankfurt, the University of Wisconsin–Milwaukee, and the University of Florida. In addition to his scholarly work, he is an active storyteller in public schools and has worked with children's theaters in France, Germany, Canada, and the United States. His major publications include *The Great Refusal: Studies of the Romantic Hero in German and American Literature* (Frankfurt, 1970), *Political Plays for Children* (St. Louis, 1976), *Breaking the Magic Spell: Radical Theories of Folk and Fairy Tales* (London, 1979), *Fairy Tales and the Art of Subversion* (New York, 1983), *The Trials and Tribulations of Little Red Riding Hood* (South Hadley, 1983), *Don't Bet on the Prince: Contemporary Feminist Fairy Tales in North America and England* (New York, 1986), *The Brothers Grimm: From Enchanted Forests to the Modern World* (1988), and *Spells of Enchantment: The Wondrous Fairy Tales of the Western World* (1991), and *Fairy Tale as Myth/Myth as Fairy Tale* (1994). Aside from writing numerous articles for journals and newspapers in the United States, Great Britain, Germany, and France, he has translated and edited *The Complete Fairy Tales of the Brothers Grimm* (1987) and is presently completing a translation of *The Fairy Tales of Hermann Hesse.*